RIDE & CRASH

MOSH SERIES BOOK 5

SUSANNA ROGERS

Bucher & Reid

ALSO BY SUSANNA ROGERS

MOSH SERIES
Holler & Howl
Down & Dirty
Slash & Burn
Light & Shade
Ride & Crash
Ground & Pound

YOUNG ADULT
Infiltration (Book 1)
Regeneration (Book 2)
Validation (Book 3)

Parallax Error

CHAPTER ONE

Cooper

Guys weren't supposed to get emotional at weddings, everyone knew that. So why the tightness in my throat, the weakness in my legs even though I was sitting down?

I knew the reason. Didn't mean the rest of the world needed to know too.

Jess leaned closer. "Nick looks so nervous."

Shifting from foot to foot, he stood down at the front, facing the white chairs that'd been laid out for the guests in his parents' enormous garden, with best man Lachie at his side.

"Don't you think, Cooper?" Jess asked more loudly.

"Yeah, sure does."

I sucked in a long, slow breath. Hell, all I had to do was make it through the ceremony and I'd be fine. It wasn't as if I was the one getting married. Besides, I'd known Nick and Lily since high school, and they had a kid together. The only surprise was that Nick had finally come to his senses and seen what had been in front of his eyes the whole time.

Meanwhile I was having a small problem with my own

eyes. Couldn't get them off the photographer. Where on earth had Nick found her? Or maybe she was a friend of Lily's. And why hadn't I already met her or at the very least seen her around?

I struggled to get a good view as the young woman crouched down near the front, camera raised, a few strands of dark hair escaping from her hairdo, the smooth skin of her neck exposed, her black dress cupping her butt. Black. For a wedding. How perfect. Black had never looked so bright or beautiful.

She straightened, tugging the skirt down with one hand, the dress clinging in all the right places. There were no wrong places.

My pulse rising, I wiped the perspiration from my brow. Nothing to do with her. I blamed the Nevada heat.

Coming to my senses, I saw Joel heading down the aisle. Our new bass player. On his own. We couldn't have that. He'd been talking to Nick and Lachie down at the front and I'd barely even noticed.

I stepped into the aisle. "Hey, why don't you join us?"

Joel stopped. "Sure."

He asked Jess if she'd prefer the aisle seat for a better view, such a gentleman. I needed to get my shit together. At the very least, I should introduce them.

"This is Jess." I laughed. "We're the leftovers."

Joel hadn't been in the band long enough to meet Jess, Lachie's girlfriend, so I explained who she was. And said I was simply left over.

She gave me a quick whack. I rubbed my shoulder. Honestly, that girl didn't know her own strength.

"No, you're not," she said. "All it means is you haven't found the right girl yet, Cooper."

Maybe she was wrong about that. I swallowed. Didn't dare turn around to look for the photographer or I'd give away too much.

Polite chat, I could do polite chat. Besides, talking about Jess and explaining how she was a bodyguard was much safer than any discussion about me. I had too much going on at the moment and wasn't ready to go there. I'd only be able to hide it for so long, though.

Glancing toward the aisle, I saw the gorgeous photographer pointing her camera in our direction.

I thrust my hand out. "No, no, thanks."

Not now. I hoped that didn't sound like panic in my voice. The band might be called The Merchants but I was absolutely not a panic merchant. I just didn't like having my photo taken so much lately.

Jess called out, and as she motioned for the young woman to join us, my heart rate rose again. And we hadn't even spoken yet. What the hell was going on with me?

"Love the dress," Jess said to her. "You look like a Korean Audrey Hepburn."

Korean, that explained the exotic looks, but what could explain that incredible combination of bombshell and demure? The breath left my body.

She left us, heading down to the front, probably preparing to take photos of the bride as she walked down the aisle.

Joel turned to Jess. "So, you know Ginger?"

"Yeah," she said. "She's a friend of my roommate's."

"And she's the official photographer?"

"Yep."

Ginger. I had a name now. And by the end of the night I hoped to have a lot more than that.

I leaned closer to Jess. "Has she always lived here?"

"Yep." She screwed up her nose. "You've been away too long."

But I was back. With a vengeance. Twenty-five years old and I'd come home to stay.

Familiar notes rang out from the piano. I knew the song. We all did. I'd wondered about the baby grand over to the side. Now I had my answer.

The chords tugged at my heart, my response immediate and undeniable. It was what music did, the reason I played in a band, even if a lot of people thought drummers weren't true musicians.

Nick, the world's biggest Paul McCartney fan, started singing *Maybe I'm Amazed*. Our singer could belt out the biggest rock songs, could do a devil's scream to rival the best, and he could melt hearts of solid metal when he sang a beautiful melody. Like now. It was enough to make a grown man cry.

We all stood as young Thomas, the ring bearer, and Lily's sister came down the aisle, followed by the bride herself. If only Nick would stop singing that song, if only the words weren't so damn meaningful, if only the melody wasn't so gut wrenching. If only…

Don't think about it, Cooper. Don't think about anything.

So I got into the zone, the strange place I took myself when things got too much for me, because there was only so much one person could cope with and I had a hell of a lot on my plate at the moment. *At the moment.* Who was I kidding? As if things were going to get better.

But I couldn't let myself mope. Refused to sulk. Hell, I'd already done enough brooding to last a lifetime.

The rest of the ceremony followed the usual plan, the

exchange of vows, the first kiss as husband and wife, then walking down the aisle together with their son, Thomas. Somehow Ginger made time between taking photos to say something to make the kid laugh and give him a fist bump.

I didn't have to wait long to congratulate the bride and groom. Nick saw me and opened his arms for a bear hug. We'd been through a lot together—as a band, as friends, and as two young guys who were constantly fucking up.

And now he was on to the next stage of his life. I held him at arm's length, my heart swelling for all the right reasons because I couldn't have been happier for him.

His lower lip trembled as he looked at me. I didn't want anything resembling pity and, besides, this was his big day. I turned to Lily instead, kissed her on both cheeks.

"I wish you every happiness," I said to her, before turning to Nick. "And you, Nick, are one lucky bastard!"

The two of them laughed.

I mingled and mixed, acting like the perfect guest. I kept an eye out for Ginger who seemed to be acting like the perfect photographer, taking plenty of photos, making Thomas giggle, giving people space when they needed it. Keeping her distance from me, it seemed too. Or maybe I was reading too much into it.

I'd give it time. Not too much, but I didn't want to annoy her when she was in full swing with the photography. Timing was everything.

Bridesmaid Scarlett came up and kissed Joel on the lips, the two of them practically radiating joyfulness. Standing nearby, I was ready to join them when a passing waiter offered me a glass of champagne.

I shook my head. "Do you have any mineral water?"

"Certainly, sir."

He came back a minute later with a San Pellegrino. I knocked back half the bottle. Must've been thirstier than I'd thought.

Yep, I told myself it was refreshing, thirst quenching, everything I could've wanted. Usually I didn't miss alcohol. This was different though, a celebration, one of those times when mineral water didn't cut it.

Joel was keen to chat since we were now in a band together, and I wanted to get to know him better too. Other people mingled while the bridal party wandered off to another part of the garden for photographs.

"This place is really something." Joel looked around.

"Yeah, isn't it?"

Nick's parents' house was a mansion, bigger than anything else I'd seen when I was growing up, the garden so large it was separated into different immaculately landscaped sections.

"I know what you mean," I said. "They've got a tennis court in their backyard. When I was a kid that used to amaze me. Still does."

"Came in handy, though."

"Sure did." They'd set the wedding marquee up on it.

Scarlett came back later, bringing Austin with her. So strange seeing the two guys together, our old bass player with the new one. Austin was happy with his decision to leave the band, with the new life he was building for himself, and especially with his new woman.

Happiness. You couldn't argue with that. What else mattered in the end?

Scarlett turned to me. "I'm on a mission. I need you to come over with us and have your photo taken. Nick wants a picture with all the guys from the band."

"Sure." I figured there'd be safety in numbers.

So we made our way to a secluded rock garden with a waterfall for the photographs.

Ginger was concentrating on the camera on its tripod, nodding and frowning at the same time, probably thinking of her next shot. Such a pretty frown. Man, I hadn't even known a frown could look so cute.

Lily waved and Nick called out, "Over here."

I joined them. We had a photo to take, and with Lachie and Austin in place next to them, I didn't want to be the one holding everybody up.

If I wasn't mistaken, Ginger was checking me out, watching me, perhaps because I'd turned down a photo before. But this was different, a group shot for old times sake. And for Lily.

We got in place for a formal photograph with the bride in the middle and two of us guys on either side.

Ginger took a couple of shots, then sized us up, a sneaky expression on her face. "Great, but can we get something that's a bit more rock 'n' roll?"

I looked at Nick, then the others, saw the glint in their eyes, and worked out exactly what they were thinking. I nodded, gave the signal, and Nick swept Lily up in his arms. She shrieked, then giggled as the four of us held her across us horizontally like something out of a teen movie. Laughing, natural, kidding around, this was 'us'.

We weren't done yet, though, Afterward, I got down on one knee, resting my arm on my leg and putting on a fake suave expression, with Lachie and Austin following suit. We'd spent enough time fooling around together to know how to ham it up.

Ginger clicked away with the camera. "Lachie, can you

come forward a bit?"

Someone handed me a rose from the garden. I put it between my teeth like a Spanish conquistador. If Ginger wanted a good pose, I'd give her one. Right now, I'd give her pretty much anything she wanted.

She gave us the thumbs up when she was done, then the three of us slowly got to our feet. I kept my distance while Ginger took more photos of the bride and groom. Lachie was talking to Joel who looked ready to explode with happiness, making me wonder what was going on.

Lachie left him and Scarlett in a rapturous hug, came over to me, and explained that Nick hadn't gotten around to telling Joel, our new bass player, he was in the band. That was one hell of an oversight. Shit, if I'd known, I'd have told him myself.

I ambled across to Joel, whacked him on the shoulder, and told him pretty much that. Scarlett had already wandered off, probably for official bridesmaid's duties, so it was just the two of us.

"There are a few other things we need to fill you in on too." I swallowed the lump in my throat. There were some things it was better not to think about. Plenty of things. I added. "Maybe another day. Now we've got to celebrate."

So we had a celebratory drink while I talked and Joel seemed to be off the planet with elation.

After a while, I made my way toward Ginger, her hand still resting on the camera, her eyes on me as I came closer. Sultry, warm, brown eyes. Beautiful pale skin tones too. I tried to keep the hunger and the ache at bay. Hard to do when her beauty stole my breath.

"Hi, Ginger." I stretched out my arm for a handshake, and cleared my throat because a trembling voice wouldn't make a good impression. "I'm Cooper McVeigh."

She squeezed my fingers, got up on tiptoes and kissed my cheek. My lips touched her cheek too. I made sure they did.

Stepping back, she looked me up and down. "I know who you are. I've seen the band."

"I hope that means you like the music."

She gave a long slow nod. "A lot."

"That's good to hear."

"You know—" she paused "—for someone who doesn't like having his photo taken, you did pretty well back there."

"I try. You caught me unawares earlier, that's all."

"I'm not like some paparazzi photographer following your every movement."

"No, I can't imagine you hiding in the bushes taking secret photos of me with a long lens while I'm taking a midnight skinny dip."

She gave me a sly smile. "I'd like to see that."

"You probably can if you Google it."

"Why would I Google when I've got the real thing in front of me?"

"Good point." I looked around. Nick and Lily were still here but most of the others had left, no doubt making their way to the reception.

Talk. I had to talk to her, keep the conversation going. "Do you do a lot of weddings?"

"A few. Mostly, I do commercial work."

"Such as?"

"Everything from advertising shots and wine bottles to headshots in boardrooms. The full range from photos of childcare centers to aged care facilities. Pretty much anything anyone will pay me to photograph." She held my gaze and smiled. "I'm fussy like that."

Despite the smooth skin and serene expression, her smile appeared loaded. And maybe a little of what lay behind those curved lips was reserved for me.

"I've taken lots of photos of local bands too," she added.

"Not The Merchants, though?"

"It was a long time ago."

"What was? You've taken photos of us?"

Shock ripped through me. Surely I'd have remembered her, unless I'd had my head well and truly up my ass or if I'd been wasted. If it was long enough ago, either of those options was a distinct possibility.

"One of your early gigs," she said. "The shots were all taken from a distance from the side of the stage or shooting through the audience. I was trying to capture the feel from the crowd. I've still got the files if you're interested."

Right now I was interested in a lot of things. I had to know more. Had to see more.

I raised my eyebrows. "Maybe you could show me sometime?"

"What? Like, come up and see my etchings? Isn't that an old line?"

"Nothing wrong with the old ways. I mean, you could email the images, but that wouldn't be quite so much fun."

"And you're all about enjoying yourself?"

"What's the point of living if you can't have a little fun from time to time?"

"True." She looked around. "But I'm working and need to move on to the reception."

"Sure."

Ginger slipped the lens cap onto the camera, crouching down while she placed it back in the camera bag and rearranged a couple of items. It gave me more of a chance to admire the curves of her hips and butt. Maybe a chance to catch my breath too.

She stood, folding the legs of the tripod and collapsing them together. Smooth, practiced movements. Long, lean legs. Toned arms and a beautiful curve to her neck. Hell, I could stand here all day.

I reached for the tripod, my hand brushing against hers. "Let me give you a hand with that."

"Ooh, I don't usually have a photographic assistant."

She handed it to me, then bent over and hoisted the camera bag over her shoulder, leaning to the other side so she didn't over balance.

"Let me take that instead," I said.

"But you're a guest."

"Come on, we'll swap." I held the tripod out to her. "I can handle it."

She bit her lip as if deliberating, then swung the camera bag in my direction. I lifted the strap over my shoulder, accidentally grunting as I did so. I didn't know how she managed with that thing. I guess that explained the muscles.

My hand on her lower back, I ushered her ahead of me. Such pretty shoulders exposed by the sleeveless dress, such a slender waist, such a gentle swing to her hips.

I'd wasted way too much time in my life doing dumb shit. Those days were over. I was turning over a new leaf, making the most of all the good things in my life, enjoying every moment.

And maybe one of those good things was right in front of me.

CHAPTER TWO

Ginger

Cooper slid down onto the seat beside mine at the reception table, passing across a flute of champagne. "I thought you might like a drink."

A sensual shiver shot up my spine that had nothing to do with the possibility of champagne and everything to do with this hunky guy.

"Thank you." I stared at the bubbles rising in the glass, tiny droplets of water condensing on the outside.

"What's up?" he asked.

"I don't usually drink when I'm working."

Not because I didn't want to, but because I had a low alcohol tolerance, which made me a cheap drunk, not necessarily a bad thing. Also, with champagne I was certain that bubbles only helped me get drunk faster.

"I thought you were nearly done for the night," he said.

"Nearly."

I picked up the glass and took a sip. Definitely didn't regret it. It tasted divine. "Wow, this is the real thing."

"Yep, Dom Perignon. Nick wouldn't skimp on a night

like tonight."

I had a few more sips because I absolutely couldn't help myself. Felt the bubbles start to do their thing, then stopped. So much for being a cheap drunk. I had the feeling that somehow tonight would end up costing me.

I pushed the glass away. "I'll finish the rest after the speeches. They're the last thing I need to shoot."

"There's also the cutting of the cake. I know how this stuff works."

As much as I loved weddings, being a guest at a wedding was one thing and being the photographer was another. Everyone else was having a ball while I was trying to get them to pose for photographs when all they wanted to do was chat with old friends.

"I hadn't forgotten about the cake." I glanced at my champagne, then at Cooper. "You're not having any?"

"Don't worry about me. I've drunk enough to last a lifetime."

"So it's true?"

"What's true?"

My face flushed. I didn't want to embarrass him but I couldn't help but notice he was the only person in the room who wasn't drinking. Except for me, that was.

I fidgeted with my napkin. "Sorry, I shouldn't read trashy magazines. I hardly ever do. Half the time reporters make things up or exaggerate. I take a lot of that stuff with a grain of salt."

"You're rambling."

"I am."

He grinned. "You're cute when you ramble."

Such a lovely smile, the sort that melted hearts, or maybe only mine.

"Look, it's okay," I said. "I can only respect that you've given up liquor. I understand how it is with alcoholics. You can't have just one glass, and that's fine."

"Me?" He placed a hand on his chest. "I was never an alcoholic. If you read that in a magazine, they got that bit wrong."

"I'm sorry." My face went redder. "But you're not drinking. And this is a wedding. It's a little unusual. I thought… "

He covered my hand with his. "I was a big drinker, no question about it, and I've seen plenty of guys do themselves damage with drinking and drugs, but I never found it hard to give that stuff up, as long as I wanted to. I just don't think I have an addictive personality."

"Well, that's good. I guess."

His expression became pained. "You're right about one thing, though. I can't even have one glass. So I won't."

So he wasn't a recovering alcoholic, but he couldn't have even one glass? I couldn't work him out.

He held my gaze. "Look, we can talk about it another time. This is a wedding. We should be celebrating."

I tilted my head. "Who said there's going to be another time?"

He squeezed my hand. "A guy can hope."

My heart swelled, my pulse rising as I looked into his pale eyes.

This wasn't going the way I'd planned. I hadn't believed my luck when Lily asked me to take their wedding photos. For lots of reasons. Because she'd seemed so lovely when we'd met to discuss the photography and I adored taking photos that made people happy, like these would.

Also because I loved The Merchants of Menace. And I wanted to take documentary photographs of the band—needed to take photos—because I couldn't have a pictorial book about the Frankston music scene without recent photos of the town's biggest export.

But none of this was turning out the way I'd thought. All those people in the crowd and my heart had fluttered as soon I'd laid eyes on Cooper. How did that work?

No wonder I'd kissed him on the cheek as soon as he'd introduced himself. As if I hadn't already known who he was. As if he hadn't already turned me into a molten mess. Well, he didn't need to know that.

I pulled away my hand, leaned back into the chair. "You'd better play your cards right then."

He gave me that suave smile again. "And you'd better start paying more attention."

"Excuse me?"

He motioned toward the front of the room. "They're just about to start the speeches."

I jumped to my feet, knocking the chair over, except Cooper grabbed it.

"Don't stress," he said. "You'll be fine."

Yep, as soon as I'd found my camera bag and was holding an actual camera, I'd be fine. I'd already scoped out the best vantage point for the speeches and got into position just in time as Nick, the man himself, picked up the microphone.

I should've been attending to my job, should never have let myself get distracted. My heart racing I crouched down, moving around to capture different angles. I kept the subject in focus, eyes sharp, with the background blurring. A few of the photos were absolute stunners, including one where Nick had his hand on his chest and Lily was out of focus beside him, caught mid-laugh.

The speeches over, I breathed a sigh of relief. I'd been concentrating so hard I couldn't even have told you what they'd said. I did a quick sweep of the room with my eyes, a habit in case there were other shots I should take. Cooper, sitting exactly where I'd left him, gave me the thumbs up. Made me smile.

Next, the cutting of the cake, a magnificent croquembouche composed of a tower of cream puffs wrapped in threads of caramel that had my mouth watering immediately. A true showstopper, except I could barely stop as I took the last of the photos of Nick and Lily cutting the cake, metaphorically speaking because there was no way they could cut into that enormous thing.

I swept the camera around the room until it rested on Cooper, his long light brown hair hanging back from his face, his brow knotted in thought. Then he spotted me, and smiled. I caught both expressions, the before and the after, wondering what they meant.

I headed for the corner where I'd stashed my camera bag because I had to put the camera away and keep my gear in a safe place. Cooper appeared while I was still crouched down, his eyes on me as I flipped the cover of the bag closed, straightening my skirt as I stood.

He sidled closer. "Jess was right."

"Sorry?"

"The dress is very Breakfast at Tiffany's."

I brushed a few strands of hair from my face. "I only wish I was half as elegant and eloquent as that particular actress."

"I haven't asked your surname yet, Ms… Hepburn?"

"It's Lee."

"Ginger Lee. You should've been an actress with a name like that."

"Are you kidding? My parents would have freaked. As it is, they want to know when I'm getting a proper job."

"What? Like a lawyer or a doctor?"

"Or an accountant," I added.

Cooper smiled. "I can't picture that."

Neither could I, which was one of the reasons my brief stint at college had been a mammoth fail. Not that my parents ever said I was a failure. They didn't need to.

"It's a cultural thing," I said. "My folks mean well."

He brushed the back of his fingers along my arm. "You know what you need? Some fresh air."

"Sure, but…"

"But what?"

I bit my lip because this was going to sound pathetic. "The cake."

He looked at me and laughed in the kindest way possible. Clearly he had no idea how much I liked my cake or my particular weakness for pastries.

I grabbed his arm. "Yep, outside."

When we reached the entrance flanked by two trees in large pots, Cooper ushered me ahead of him, his hand in the small of my back. I liked these little touches, the way they made me feel petite and alluring.

After leaving the air conditioned marquee, the warmth of the summer evening made the back of my neck prickle as the night air seeped into my skin.

"Don't you love it here?" I wandered away from the entrance.

"Sure do."

He took my hand, leading me around the corner to the side of the marquee near a fence that cordoned off the tennis court. Not the most scenic spot. And not that I cared.

I looked up at the night sky and crescent moon. "I meant Frankston, the city, the people, the way things happen here."

"I agree. This place is home. Always will be. My family is here, my best friends, not much else compares with that."

"What about playing Lollapalooza with a hundred thousand adoring fans? Or even the Flats Festival?"

He grinned. "Well, yeah, that stuff's amazing. Can't deny it."

I gazed into his eyes. "You know, at first when you didn't want your photo taken, I was afraid you might be the tortured artist type."

A hand on his chest, he laughed. "Me?"

"I've photographed lots of bands in town, met a lot of musicians, and most of them are really nice."

"That's good to hear."

"But so often, there's one guy who lets everyone down. The singer who thinks he's a rock star. Or the guitar player who thinks everyone came to the gig to see him do his didly-didly guitar riffs."

I contorted my face, playing some air guitar to make my point.

He laughed. "Or who does 'guitar face' when he's playing?"

"Exactly."

"You look very cute when you do that, by the way."

"I haven't finished yet. Or the guy who's hooked on

smack and ends up selling someone else's guitars to buy drugs."

"The Merchants had one of those. He got kicked out of the band before they made it big. That's how I got the gig. Best thing that ever happened to me." Cooper nodded. "You really do know a lot about the dynamics of bands."

I held his gaze. "You're not like that but somehow I keep coming back to that word. Tortured."

Something glimmered in his eyes, maybe some pain from his past. I had my own pain too, my own loss from long ago, this one thing that stayed with me.

Then Cooper cupped my jaw in his hands, tilting my head higher, and all rational thought left me.

"The only thing that's torture," he said, "is standing here in front of you and not kissing you."

He pressed his lips softly against mine and, for a moment, I felt as if I was looking down on the two of us, the properly-raised Korean girl being kissed by the cool guy with the long hair. The girl whose dreams were coming true. Who'd never even imagined this, not until a few hours ago.

I floated back down to earth. No, this guy wasn't a fantasy. He was standing in front of me and very much real.

His next kiss was gentle, teasing, testing, but I didn't want gentle. I wanted all of him. Could he see the hunger in my eyes? Was the same desire simmering deep in his belly too?

I slid my hands up to his shoulders, my head tilted, lips parted. His hands on my waist, he pulled me close and threw us into a kiss that left me with no doubt. He pushed me up against the fence, his tongue rolling against mine, hands wandering over my waist, my hips. My chest was heaving against his, my breasts crushed. Damn it, I wanted his hands everywhere.

Breathless, we gave ourselves some space, staring into each other's eyes. I needed air. I needed Cooper.

"We should go inside," I said.

"We can do that." He took my hand. "For now."

I stepped inside the marquee ahead of him, forced myself to get my head together, then noticed waiters clearing the dirty plates and serving coffee. By the look of it, wedding cake had been served, consumed, and finished. My loss. Not that I felt I'd lost out under the circumstances.

I sucked in a deep breath, leaned closer to Cooper. "I need to check on a couple of things."

"Sure."

The number one thing I had to do was check with Nick and Lily that I had all the shots they needed. Number two was go to the bathroom. And number three … I couldn't even remember what that was. I chatted with a couple of people on my way back from the bathroom, tried to act natural and probably did a reasonable job.

Yesterday the main thing on my mind had been getting in good with the band so they'd agree to a series of documentary photos for the book. I didn't want just a couple of shots. It had to be a full suite. The book needed to revolve around them or it wouldn't work.

But I didn't want to bring that up now. Didn't want Cooper to think that was why I'd kissed him when the only reason I needed was sitting at the table waiting for me to return.

I should check my camera bag one last time before I sat down—a habit because my livelihood depended on my camera gear. I pressed the plastic latches, pulled open the flap, checked inside the bag, and did a double take.

Nestled in a compartment next to my camera bag was a clear plastic container with several cream puffs from the croquembouche. Who'd left them there? Cooper or perhaps Lily?

As soon as I caught Cooper's gaze, he shrugged, then threw his hands up, looking around as if innocent. I let out a long sigh. If I wasn't in love before, I sure as hell was now.

I couldn't wipe the smile from my face as I made my way back to the table. "How did you know?"

He spread his arms. "How could I not know? You swooned when you laid eyes on that towering cake."

My eyes narrowed, my lips thinning. "I did not! I was working. There was no time for me to be staring or swooning or whatever you're suggesting."

"Only for a second but I saw you."

I folded my arms. "I don't know what you mean."

My serious face could only last so long. Cooper cracked a smile and we both burst out laughing.

Settling back into his chair, he got that faraway look I'd seen earlier. It was part of my job to be observant and I'd already spent way too much time observing him today.

"It's funny, you know," I said. "Sometimes you look lost and other times you seem so certain."

He leaned back in his chair. "Maybe I'm an enigma."

"Ooh, that's a big word."

"It's not true, either. I'm just a guy."

"Yeah, a guy who plays in one of the biggest rock

bands in the country."

His face clouded over. "Something like that."

Why would he seem so reluctant when it came to the band? Playing in The Merchants was a huge achievement, one he should be proud of. And I'm sure he was.

He reached under the table, taking my hand into his, my skin sizzling from the warmth of his touch. My fingers trembled as I pulled his hand onto my thigh. I wanted more. Didn't want our night to finish here.

A moment later, his lips were nuzzling inside my neck. Not a friendly kiss on the cheek. No, this was much more. I edged away, suddenly alert, aware we were in a room full of people even if the crowd had thinned.

I waited a moment. "I'm kind of reserved."

"Really?"

"I'm not into public displays of affection. I mean, it's different if two people are in a relationship but we've only just met."

"What about *private* displays of affection?"

A shiver shot up my spine, my lips curving to a smile. "Now that's a different thing altogether."

"You could come back to my place for a drink if you like."

My breath caught in my throat. This went against everything I believed. Never in my life had I gone home with a guy I'd just met. Not that I judged people who went for one-night stands, only that they weren't right for me. I liked to get to know a guy better. A lot better.

How could I even be thinking about this? Except I wasn't thinking about it. I was well and truly decided, my pulse racing, desire burning deep in my belly.

"I'll leave first," I said.

Eyes narrowing, he tapped a finger on the side of his nose. "Then no one would suspect anything was going on."

"I just mean…" I couldn't help thinking it'd be blatantly obvious to anyone who was looking that something was going on between us. "I'm supposed to be a professional."

A gleam in his eyes. "And I'm looking forward to you showing me those photographs we were talking about, if not tonight, then another time."

I swallowed. I'd be showing him a lot more than my etchings. Maybe this wouldn't be a one-night stand after all, because that'd be the only thing about the evening that was a mistake.

One night wouldn't be enough. Not with a guy like him. Not nearly enough.

CHAPTER THREE

Cooper

My place, her place, it didn't really matter to me as long as Ginger was happy. I slid the key into the door and stepped inside, turning to take her hand into mine.

I deposited the camera bag inside the living room, glad to take that particular weight off my shoulders, and switched on the floor lamp in the corner, bathing the room in a soft glow.

I hoped she liked the place. Big leather sofas and bright rugs weren't to everyone's taste. White walls showed off my artworks, big colorful things in burnt orange and deep burgundy to match the rug. Not that I knew anything about art, only what I liked.

And I liked what I saw in front of me.

Sidling up beside Ginger, I slid my hands onto her waist and pressed my lips against her neck. Such an attractive curve to her neck. Sleek and svelte, like the rest of her.

She turned around, stayed close. "Isn't this the bit where you offer me a drink? Then again, maybe not. I mean, not if you're not drinking too."

"I make a mean hot chocolate," I said.

Her face lit up. "What a coincidence, I love hot chocolate."

"Ah, one more thing." I crouched by her camera bag, flipped open the lid, and pulled out the plastic container I'd placed there earlier. "These should go in the fridge."

Her eyes widened, perhaps at the sight of the cream puffs or perhaps at what I was implying. Because I was hoping like hell those pastries would stay in the fridge for hours and hours while she stayed the night.

"Sure." She came with me to the kitchen.

This room had sold me on the house. The other places I'd looked at had modern, white kitchens that were way too shiny and sparkling whereas this one had wooden cupboards and ample room for a chunky Oregon table in the middle. Besides, I hated white and liked homely. When it came to kitchens anyway.

I put the kettle on while Ginger looked around some more.

"Do you cook much?" she asked.

"A little. I need all the help I can get in that department." I reached inside the pantry for a packet. "Marshmallows?"

"On the side, please." She smiled. "I'm surprised you've got marshmallows, a grown man like you."

"I got them for Thomas, Nick's boy, when they came over the other day."

"Great." She threw her hands up. "I've got the same tastes as a four-year-old."

I pulled her close. "I hope not."

Tilting her chin up with one hand, I covered her mouth with mine, felt the softness of her lips, felt a lot of other things going on in my body.

The shrill cry of the kettle cut through the air. I broke off the kiss. We had time. We had all night. I hoped.

I tipped a heaping spoon of cocoa and two spoons of sugar into each mug, then poured in hot water, mixed furiously, and added a generous amount of milk.

"Um, that was nice of you," Ginger said. "Buying marshmallows for Thomas, that is."

I placed three marshmallows on a side plate. "I'm not as nice as you think."

I'd cleaned up my act a few years ago, a distinct turning point in my life. A near death experience can do that to you, one that I'd brought upon myself by getting behind the wheel drunk. Talk about selfish and stupid and generally a shitty thing to do. Still, it could've turned out a lot worse.

I'd been such a prick back then that sometimes I still couldn't believe the other guys in the band had put up with me. Maybe the only reason they had was because I was better than their old drummer.

Ginger picked up her mug. "Of course you're a good guy. I wouldn't be here if you weren't."

"My deep, dark secrets aren't that much of a secret. A lot of the shit I did made it into those trashy magazines you haven't read." I waited a moment. "Did you know I got married in Vegas at twenty-two? Then got divorced a few months later."

She nodded. "Yeah, I read about it. That's younger than me. I'm twenty-three."

"I don't do that sort of crazy shit anymore. I'm a better person than that now."

'Crazy' was an understatement. Lucy thought she was

Courtney and I was Kurt, minus the intravenous drugs, probably the only stupid thing we didn't do. Hell, I shouldn't even have brought the subject up, except for this strange need I felt to get things in the open. Some things anyway.

Sweeping up my mug and the marshmallows, I led the way back into the living room where we settled onto the sofa.

Sitting forward, Ginger blew on her hot chocolate and took a sip. "This is good."

"Told you so."

She munched her way through the marshmallows, examining each one before taking a bite, deep in concentration before she got back to her hot chocolate. I could sit here all night and watch her. I didn't even mind the silence between us. Quite liked it in fact.

After a while, she said, "You're different from the other guys in the band."

I sipped my drink. "Not really. Austin always felt he was different because he's a bit older and was into rockabilly."

"Is that why he left?"

"Yes. No." How to explain this? "He had a different dream from the rest of us so he bit the bullet and went back to architecture. I think he may have felt left out because Nick, Lachie, and I went to high school together, and then I joined the band a bit later on."

"A lot has happened since then."

"Sure has." I slid my hand onto her knee. "Would you like me even if I wasn't in The Merchants?"

"What kind of question is that? Of course I would." A little furrow formed in her brow. "You're not leaving the band too, are you?"

"Why would I do that?"

My throat tightened. The only way I coped was by not thinking about it, and I had the world's best distraction in front of me.

Desire coursed through me. That was more like it.

"Sorry," she said. "Maybe I've read too many of those trashy magazines."

"You could end up in one, you know." I held my hand out. "Your photo on the front page. I can see the headlines. *Look Who's Cooped up With Cooper.*"

She covered her mouth. "Oh, no, that's terrible."

"I'm only joking. Far as I know, there aren't any paparazzi following us. No spy cameras set up inside." My eyes narrowed. "Unless *you're* the paparazzo."

"Me? No way. We've been through that."

I kissed her nose. "That's right. You're a professional. With a sweet tooth."

"Well, I'm not working at the moment." She sipped her hot chocolate. "You know, I wasn't sure what to expect before I got here. At first I was afraid you might live in some student dive."

"Nope, been there, done that."

"Then I thought you might have some fancy hi-tech place like Tony Stark's Malibu mansion."

"In Frankston?"

"Well, something like that. But this place doesn't say 'rock star' or 'rich dude'. It feels like a home. Did you use an interior decorator?"

I took that as a compliment. "No, I had a pretty good idea what I wanted and the band has been back for a few months so I had the time."

And also the need to set myself up so I'd be comfortable. Because now that I was back, I wasn't going anywhere.

I still hoped to play The Salt Flats Festival in a couple of months—if things went to plan—and we had a shitload of recording to do in the meantime because we'd been spectacularly good at procrastinating. After that, the guys would get back to touring even if they were planning on changing things around and doing shorter tours so they could spend more time at home.

It was enough to wrench the heart from my chest. The band was everything to me. Everything.

Ginger bounced on the sofa, exactly the distraction I needed.

"Your furniture's so new," she said.

"It'll get worn in."

In fact, we could start on that right now. I took the mug from her hand, placing it on the coffee table. My lips touched hers. She tasted of chocolate. I needed more than one small taste.

Reclining her back onto the sofa, I wrapped my arms around her and kissed her. She fit so well against me, her body molding against mine, her hands tugging at the back of my neck.

Sliding out from under me, she sat on the edge of the sofa, struggling with the zipper on the back of her dress. Cute and sexy without even trying.

"I can help with that."

Sidling closer, I inched the zipper down, her back arching against my touch. I nuzzled into her neck, peppering the bare skin with little kisses, sliding one bra strap down over her shoulder, then the other. Ginger gasped, a beautiful sound.

"I've never done this before," she said in a low voice. "Stayed the night on a first date, that is."

I kissed her again, my hands covering her breasts, except the bra and the damn dress were still in my way.

"This isn't a date," I whispered.

Her little hands on my chest, she pushed me away, her mouth open as she stared.

I grinned. "I'm only teasing." Her shoulders relaxed so I added, "We can go on a proper date, tomorrow, the next day, whenever you like. I've got plenty of time, Ginger."

My heart twisted because that was only half true, even though the sentiment was one hundred percent sincere. I wanted her like I'd never wanted anyone before. And that wasn't just my dick talking.

She raised her eyebrows. "Really?"

I nodded. "Really."

Her lips curved to a smile. "I'm free for a few days. I don't have any jobs booked till Wednesday."

She unbuttoned my shirt slowly, peeling it from my shoulders to toss it to the floor. Her eyes wandered over the tattoos that covered my arms and shoulders, then she followed with her fingers, her touch light and inquisitive.

Her lips parted as she stood, sliding off the dress so it slipped to the floor, her pale skin glowing against the black of her underwear.

And I fell. Falling harder than I'd ever fallen before as she reached behind to unclasp her bra, then slipped out of her panties.

I stood, reaching for her hand. "The bedroom."

She shook her head slowly, stepping away and sliding down onto the rug. Leaning back on her hands, she beckoned me with her eyes. Other parts of her body were beckoning too, her nipples practically calling out for me to take them into my mouth, that lush body waiting to be kissed, those hips ready to lie under mine.

She brought the tip of her tongue to her lips. "Who needs a bed?"

And who was I to argue?

When it came to Ginger Lee, I'd take anything I could get.

CHAPTER FOUR

Ginger

Talk about whirlwind. At least my fears about a one-night stand hadn't come true, though at the moment this could possibly have turned to a five-night stand. Not that I was counting.

I'd got through Wednesday's job, some boardroom shots for a legal firm, and so far those three hours had been the most time I'd spent apart from Cooper since we'd met. Naturally after that, we'd had to make up for lost time.

Today it was wine bottles in the studio, the job tricky in its own way because my photographic studio was at my parents' place. Their double garage, to be more precise. Maybe it was too soon. Or too late. I wasn't sure which.

Cooper picked up one of the wine bottles, wiping it clean of dust and fingerprints before handing it to me.

I placed the bottle carefully in position on the table where I was shooting. "Looks like I've got you well trained."

"No problem. I didn't even know we had much of a wine business here," he said, his voice strained.

"Nevada's not exactly the Napa Valley but the industry is growing."

Cooper wasn't himself today, his skin pale and lines bracketing his mouth appearing out of nowhere.

"Why don't you take a seat?" I suggested.

"Sure." He sat down, leaning forward with his arms resting on his thighs. The guy just couldn't help but look rugged. "Pretty good set-up you've got here. It was nice of your parents to offer you their garage."

"Yeah, they jumped in to help a couple of years back. As soon as I'd mentioned how expensive studio rental was, in fact."

Which was ironic because they still wanted to know when I was going to get a proper job. They were disappointed when I dropped out of college but, as much as I'd tried, I couldn't follow in my brother's footsteps and become an accountant. I'd been fooling myself.

That'd been the first 'big' disappointment. After that, I moved out of my home before getting married. An enormous no-no for my very traditional mother who knew how the relatives in Korea would look upon this. I think my parents had given up on me after that.

Still, I appreciated the use of the studio-slash-garage. It had its own entry, aside from the roller doors that were permanently locked and largely hidden by wide rolls of backdrop.

My phone pinged so I turned to check it, biting my lip as I saw the message.

"What's up?" Cooper asked.

"Nothing." I smiled. "My mom's on her way."

I usually texted her when I was using the studio, as a courtesy, and I'd explained to her about Cooper because she was a huge fan of The Merchants and would never have forgiven me.

It felt weird for her to be meeting him so soon but the alternative would've been worse. She'd already told me off for bringing him to the studio on her day off when she had a weekly lunch date at her favorite café with the girls.

Butterflies fluttered in my stomach that had nothing to do with my mother. I'd been procrastinating about asking if The Merchants would take part in the book I was putting together. Maybe my life didn't depend on it but sometimes it felt that way.

Cooper placed a hand on my waist. "Why so nervous?"

"I'm not. I'm concentrating."

Leaning over, I looked through the viewfinder, then reached forward to turn the bottle slightly. I kept my set-up simple because otherwise everything would end up getting reflected in the bottle, and the pictures needed to look sleek. A single soft box for light and a big sheet of white polystyrene foam as a reflector, that was all I used, keeping the light box and the poly very close together and then shooting through a slit at the front. For red wine, that was. Whites reflected the light differently.

I got the shot, stood back.

"That's it?" Cooper asked.

"Yep."

The previous images had taken longer while I'd leaned over the bottles with a piece of white card, trying to get the reflections in foils just right. Designers loved using metallics on their labels. Unfortunately they reflected lots of light, and I had to make sure the labels were still readable.

Cooper got up and placed his hands on my hips from behind, leaving a little kiss on my neck.

I slapped his hand. "Hey."

"Sorry, you're concentrating and I keep forgetting." He couldn't keep the smile from his voice. "You're a professional."

Also, my mother could walk in at any moment, the thought of which made me feel like a recalcitrant teenager all over again.

A knock at the door. That'd be her now. I rushed to pull the door open but she stepped in before I got there, her eyes fixated on the only other person in the room.

As stunning as always, Mom waltzed in, the skirt of her Anne Klein dress floating behind her, a cute bolero thrown over her shoulders. No Old Navy for her. Suddenly I felt underdressed in my ripped jeans.

"Cooper, this is my mom, Michelle," I said, as he walked up to meet her.

He shook her hand. "You know, I could've guessed this was your mom. You've got the same eyes and face shape, even the same smile."

She looked at me as I placed my camera inside its bag, securing the flap shut. "You're not leaving, are you?"

"We're pretty much done here," I said.

"But your brother is on his way."

I raised my eyebrows. "What? Shouldn't he be at work?"

She planted her hands on her hips. "He's just popping out of the office to say hello, that's all. Alistair's a fan. You can't blame him."

"No problem," Cooper said. "We can hang around a bit longer."

I held his gaze. "But you said you were tired."

I had a feeling Cooper was coming down with something. He seemed to be forcing himself through everything he did today. Except for kissing me. He seemed to have energy for that.

"But I'd love to meet your brother," he said.

My phone pinged again. Alistair.

I'm just around the corner.

"I know what Cooper needs," Mom said. "Some jasmine tea."

He nodded. "That'd be lovely, thanks."

Mom gave his shoulder a squeeze. "I'll be right back."

A minor commotion played outside the door as Mom left and my brother arrived, beaming before he'd even walked through the door.

Alistair raced across to shake Cooper's hand while I did the introductions.

"I'm a huge fan." My brother's eyes couldn't have been wider. "I've got all your albums and there's a new one coming up."

Cooper nodded. "That's right. We've started working on it but we've got a long way to go."

"And you're recording it here?"

"Yep. Getting back to our roots. Besides, Masterson's Studio is up there with the best in the world. In my humble opinion, anyway."

"Could I get a photo with you?" Alistair asked. "For my Instagram."

Cooper shrugged. "Sure."

Alistair dug his phone out from his pocket and passed it to me. I took several shots to make sure I got the best expressions.

Mom came in, the refreshing smell of jasmine tea wafting through the air as she passed a cup to Cooper and he sat back down. She and Alistair sat side by side on the only two other chairs in the studio, alternating between admiring the photos on the phone and staring at the real thing.

"When Mom told me you were going to be here, I didn't believe her," Alistair said to Cooper. He turned to me. "Why didn't you say anything?"

"I told you I was shooting Nick and Lily's wedding."

"But you didn't tell me the two of you were such good friends."

"I've been busy."

And somehow I'd known Alistair would make a fuss and I'd end up feeling uncomfortable whereas, strange as it seems, I knew Mom would take it more in her stride.

Cooper looked at my mom, then at me. "You've got very good genes in your family. If you're lucky, you'll end up looking like your mom one day."

"Such a compliment, thank you." A smile tugged at the corners of Mom's lips. "But will you be around to see what my daughter looks like when that happens?"

Perhaps she wasn't as cool about this as I'd thought. Embarrassment shot through me, my face reddening.

"It's a bit soon for that, Mom," I said. "We've only just started dating."

Cooper settled back into his chair. "Actually, I'd love to see how good Ginger's going to look, but I don't know if I'll be around. We don't know if any of us will be around."

Mom nodded. "That's true, Cooper, so true."

The words would be bringing back somber memories

for her, something Cooper couldn't know. Alistair may have gotten over childhood cancer many years ago but Mom was still scarred by it. I was scarred too, not so much about Alistair because I'd only been ten at the time and the severity of his illness hadn't sunk in, not properly.

It had been different with Mitch. At seventeen, I had well and truly understood. He hadn't gotten over it. And the pain had cut me through to my core.

"I gotta say, it's lovely to meet your family," Cooper said. "What about your dad?"

"He's at work," I said, "where Alistair is supposed to be."

My brother looked up. "Nothing wrong with doing the nine-to-five thing. Some of us have to work."

"Okay, you two." Mom stood. "Ginger, can you give me a hand in the kitchen?"

I knew what that was code for, so we left the boys to it and I followed my mom outside. We didn't even make it inside the house, just wandered to the front porch.

"He seems very nice even if he's not Korean," she said.

"Mom, even I'm not *that* Korean. I was born here, remember?"

"Yes, I was there at the time." Mom could be very dry when she wanted to.

Sometimes she struggled with being stuck between two worlds. She'd come to America from Korea at age five and had been raised in a very traditional family, and had then married a Korean man—not because she had to, but because she'd fallen in love—only Dad was as American as they came.

"Maybe I'm a little starstruck." She smiled, didn't seem

offended, then grew serious as she reached for my hand. "Honey, I like him, that's not the problem. But I don't want you to get hurt. I can see where this is headed. Getting involved with a guy like him isn't going to work. He won't marry you, won't settle down, won't give you the things you need."

My stomach clenched. So we were doomed before we'd started? I didn't want to think about that, didn't want it to be true.

"Mom, I'm not going to marry him. We've only just started dating."

And I'd barely come out of the closet about the relationship. We'd been so cloistered in our own little world, just the two of us together day and night, that even him meeting my family seemed like a big step.

I breathed a small sigh of relief. Maybe that part hadn't been so bad after all, despite the current mother-daughter discussion.

"You're twenty-three," Mom said.

"I know." Only two years off twenty-five, the not-so-magical age after which I'd be considered to be left on the shelf.

"You've had lots of boyfriends."

"Yeah."

"But something's different. I can feel it. That's why I'm concerned. He's not like the others."

"I'd never let myself end up in a bad position, Mom." Except for that one time we hadn't been quite so careful. Feeling the color come to my face, I quickly gave her a hug. "You don't need to worry so much. And I need to get going."

Stepping toward the garage, she pulled the door open

for me. "Okay, honey."

As soon as I laid eyes on Cooper in the studio, it reminded me I still had to talk to him about my book. Not that I was procrastinating. Much. A fresh wave of nerves shot through me.

I'd do it now, I decided, right away.

Alistair helped carry the wine bottles and some of my gear out to the car, chatting amicably as if it was no trouble at all. He seemed to be turning into the perfect brother now I had Cooper around. Mom gave my hand a squeeze before we got into the car.

It wasn't far from my parents' place to my apartment, so I started talking before I changed my mind, explaining to Cooper about the book. And the photos. And the band.

I pulled up outside my apartment block. I liked the place because from the outside it looked like a motel from a 1950s movie, a two-story building with a parking lot and a couple of palm trees out front, and on the inside it was a blank slate.

Cooper sat beside me on the front seat, his expression even, not giving much away. My heart dropped. I'd been hoping for some excitement on his part or at the very least some sign of interest.

"I understand you're not always wild about having your picture taken," I said. "But the photos won't be obtrusive. It won't be like having your photo taken with my brother."

"It's not that." He reached across to stroke my arm. "The timing is really bad."

"But you guys are here until The Salt Flats Festival, maybe longer, you said."

"It's ... complicated."

I gazed into his eyes, tried not to let my disappointment show. Deep down I'd known this was going to be a problem, even if I didn't understand why.

"I'll think about it," he said. "I want to help, truly I do."

I reached down to pop the trunk, then got out of the car. The other guys in the band weren't the problem. No, I knew exactly where the problem lay.

Cooper raced around to the back of the car before I got there. "Just give me a couple of days, and I'll see what I can do."

"Sure." I kept my voice even.

He slid his hands onto my waist, made me feel small and wanted, even if I wasn't sure exactly what was going on with him.

"Is that why you seemed so nervous today?" he asked.

"That, and this whole meeting-the-family-thing."

"Why would that be a problem? Your family is lovely."

Cooper and I had been seeing so much of each other, practically living in each other's pockets, and now there were these other people involved.

I threw my hands up. "I don't know, maybe I didn't want to jinx things."

He grinned, the smile reaching his eyes as he pressed a gentle kiss to my lips. He was right about me being anxious today but I wasn't exactly telling the truth.

I'd been through a lot, perhaps more than other people my age—with my brother's illness, with Mitch, with life in general. And, as my mother had pointed out, I'd had plenty of boyfriends and I'd been in love before.

But not like this.

CHAPTER FIVE

Cooper

Hard to believe it'd been nearly two weeks since Nick and Lily's wedding, or since I'd met Ginger, to be more precise. I had no clue what'd happened in the preceding two weeks whereas with Ginger around, it felt as if everything had happened.

Meanwhile poor old Nick had only been back from his honeymoon a couple of days and he'd come crashing down to earth with renovations at The Swamp in the final stages and band rehearsals in full swing.

I reached across with the drum key to tune the snare. "Must be hard for you, Nick."

"What?" He looked up, his long hair falling back from his face.

"Leaving Lily when you're all loved up at home."

"Ha." He raised his eyebrows. "You can talk!"

Smirking, I tested the snare. It sounded right. Yep, we were all back home again and in our element here at Masterson's Studio.

The place had been updated since we'd cut our first album here, complete with shiny new rehearsal rooms that were a far cry from some of the shitty places we used to rehearse. Soundproofed and clean, these rooms didn't smell like beer, vomit, or cigarette smoke, making this a huge step up from the old days.

And now we had Joel, the main reason for these rehearsal sessions. The rest of us had played together for years and were a tight unit. The only way to get to that stage was by rehearsing and practicing together. A lot. Shortcuts didn't work, and we took what we did very seriously.

Lachie had his back to us, fiddling with his amp and the pedals on the floor.

"How's the new love of your life?" I yelled.

He turned around. "Sorry?"

"Your new Gretsch? How are the two of you getting on?"

He grinned. "Hey, no one's allowed to make fun of the White Falcon. Have you heard how good this thing sounds?"

He strummed a few chords.

"We all have." I had to admit it did sound amazing.

"I like to think of this as—" he plucked a string "—the newest member of the band."

"Um," Joel interrupted. "I thought that was me."

"Don't worry," I said. "You're more important than the Gretsch. And if Nick ever gets a signature guitar, you'll be more important than that too."

Nick grunted. "Yeah, *if.*"

A sore point because he was itching for a Nick Steel model guitar, acoustic or electric, he didn't mind. He kept hoping, and it was our job to keep giving him shit about it. It's what friends were for.

No one gave me a hard time though, not even when I'd been at my worst a couple of years ago. I'd been angry as all hell, furious at the world, at myself, at anyone who came near me. It'd been one of the stages I'd gone through. Even then, the guys had been understanding with me.

I swallowed back the regret. It was part of my past.

Joel tuned his bass and I practiced a fill on the drums, then stopped for a bit so he could hear what he was doing. Rehearsals were always a bit of a mess. Until we got going, that was.

"Ginger is coming soon," I said after the noise levels settled down. "As soon as I message her, that is."

"Sure," Nick said. "She can hang around. Might get a bit boring for her, though."

"That's not it." I swallowed. "There's something she wants to ask us but I said I'd discuss it with you guys first."

Nick strummed his guitar. "Ask us what?"

So I told them about her plans for publishing a photo book of Frankston bands and how she particularly wanted to document The Merchants.

I added the line about how no book about Frankston music would be complete without us, not because the guys needed flattering but because it was true. Nick and Lachie both nodded, didn't say much, looked reserved.

"She's taken heaps of photos of local bands," Joel said. "She doesn't interfere, just stays in the background and does her thing. It's fine by me if she wants to make a record of what we're doing."

Lachie chewed on the guitar pick between his lips while Nick leaned on his amplifier, silence resonating through the room.

Joel looked around. "Did I say something wrong?"

"Nah, not at all," I said.

"Is it because I'm the new guy?"

"Nope." I held his gaze. "You're part of the band and don't you forget it."

Nick cleared his throat. "There's stuff you don't know."

Panic ripped through me. No, surely he wasn't going to tell him now. I wasn't ready, hadn't psyched myself up for it. Besides, when the time came, *I'd* have to be the one to tell him.

Hell, I probably should have explained the situation already, but he hadn't been with us very long and I was still getting to know him. I liked the guy, his work ethic, his attitude, the way he'd just stuck up for Ginger. And for me.

But it didn't feel right, not when I hadn't told Ginger yet. My heart clenched, my throat tight. Why did life have to be so hard?

"We went through this about a year ago," Nick said. "Some guy approached us backstage at a music festival. He was a bit of a prick, kept name dropping—as if that was going to impress us—and said he wanted to tour with us for a month, taking photos. We turned him down."

Joel nodded. "Oh, okay."

I gave Nick a pointed look. "Things have moved on since then. It'd be different with Ginger taking the photos. I really want to do this."

Nick frowned. "Are you sure this is what you want?"

I nodded.

Lachie shrugged. "Well, if it's okay by Cooper then I don't have a problem with it."

"I take it that's a yes." I looked around at each of the guys. "It'd mean a lot to me to have these photos taken, while we're all young and making music, doing what we love. While we're all here."

"Better than waiting till we're old and our faces are lined and craggy," Joel said.

I whacked the snare. "Exactly."

"Not that I'm criticizing The Stones," he added. "Brilliant band, lots of wrinkles, that's all I'm saying."

Wrinkles didn't seem so bad. If we made it that far. My heart lurched.

Nick strummed his guitar. "Then we should get on with it."

My phone pinged so I checked it. "Ginger's in the parking lot."

Nick paused, held my gaze for a moment. "Then let her in, dude."

I held the door open and watched as Ginger approached. Even the camera bag dragging down one shoulder barely slowed her down. The sight of her made me overflow with joy, more than I had in a long time. Since she'd entered my life, I always seemed to be overflowing with something.

She kissed me on the lips, then stepped inside. "Hi, guys."

"Make yourself comfortable," Nick said. "We've already played around enough. Time to get moving, guys."

Ginger raised her eyebrows. "So I can stay?"

I smiled. "You can pick up your camera anytime you like."

Nick grinned. "Make sure you capture my good side."

Her eyes wide, Ginger couldn't stop beaming. Nick

was already letting loose with a guitar riff so I motioned to the chair behind me.

Nick let rip with a devil's scream, which told us which song this was. *Holler.* I only hoped Joel could keep up. Guitar first, then the drums and bass came in after that. I nodded at him a split second before it was time to come in. Spot on.

At the end of the song, we all looked around the room at each other.

"A great first effort." Nick turned to Joel. "Let's do it again. Play it straighter this time. Don't try to swing it."

Joel nodded. "No problem."

So we played it again. And again. And again. Getting a bit tighter each time.

Energy surged through me. I'd felt strong as soon as I'd woken up this morning and had known it was going to be a good day, not a feeling I had very often nowadays.

It mixed with the desperation that clawed away inside me whenever I played because every time could be the last. Because I wanted this. Because the band meant so much to me.

I didn't pay Ginger much attention. And that was saying something because normally I was very aware of her presence. She was like a fly on the wall. Barely there.

After a while, we took a break. I knocked back a bottle of water and joined Ginger in the corner of the room. I was happy to stand and stretch my legs after spending so much time sitting, while the other three guys took the opportunity to sit down.

Ginger gave me a quick kiss on the lips. "You shouldn't come and talk to me."

"I shouldn't?" I asked.

"No, you're part of the band. You're supposed to be relaxing with the other guys."

I slid my hand onto her hip, nuzzling into her neck. "I'm relaxed."

She smiled. "I'll let you off this time but we've been through this."

"Yep, no problem. I'll be better behaved next time."

We took what we did seriously and so did Ginger. She wanted to capture us as we were, acting as we normally would during a rehearsal, whether we were joking around or concentrating on the songs or even arguing. While she was shooting, this wasn't about me and her.

"Are you guys ready?" I called out. "Bunch of slackers, sitting around like that."

Lachie pointed to the drum kit. "You can talk. All you do is sit around."

I stood, picked up my drumsticks as if ready to throw them. "Remember, I've got weapons."

The others got to their feet, took up their instruments, and we got back into it. Business as usual. That was one of the things I loved about this, the fact I could lose myself in it. Nick and Lachie got a bit bored with rehearsals sometimes because they had the rather more exotic job of writing songs for the band too. This was plenty exotic enough for me.

Another hour or two in, it started to hit me, exhaustion seeping into my bones, an overwhelming tiredness that sunk deep down, my joints aching. The doctors called it fatigue but somehow that didn't seem to cover it. Didn't get close.

Nick switched off his amp. "I reckon we should call it a day."

He knew me too well or maybe he simply recognized that we'd been at it a long time.

Joel nodded. "Good, because I'm toast."

It must be hard being the newest member of the band, the one who was still getting comfortable with the songs when the rest of us had been doing this for years. And it was a relief to have Joel as an excuse.

"The songs sound great, guys!" Ginger yelled, the first thing she'd said since our break.

"Thanks," I said.

Nick placed his guitar back in its case. "I'd better get back to Lily and Thomas."

Lachie packed his effects pedals into a bag, looked across at Joel. "Have you got time to come back to my place? To work on those songs."

"Sure."

Lachie turned to me. "You don't need a hand with the drum kit, do you?"

"Nah, it's staying."

They were leaving their amplifiers here too because we'd be back again tomorrow. Their instruments were a different matter. No way would Lachie leave his treasured Gretsch unattended. He hadn't had that thing very long but he loved it.

The other guys left in a hurry so it was just me and Ginger.

She came up to me in the middle of the room, took my hands into hers. "How'd I do?"

"You did good. I hate to say it but sometimes I forgot you were there."

"That's wonderful." Her eyes widened, then she held my gaze. "So it's true? I've got the gig?"

"You sure do."

Still holding my hands, she did a little dance, her whole face lighting up. Sometimes she looked like she was three years old. Then, as she lifted her gaze to meet mine, she was all woman again.

I didn't know how she did it. Ten minutes ago, the only thing I'd felt was exhausted. Now I felt something else as desire surged through my veins, blood rushing through my body, to one part in particular. Damn it, I wanted her.

Sliding my hands along her jaw, I cupped her face in my hands, brought my mouth crashing over hers. Not gentle, no way, that wasn't how I felt.

I turned and left her, only for a moment, because one of us had to lock the door. She stayed where she was, her lips parted, gazing at me through eyes that were narrowing with desire. Bedroom eyes, except there wasn't a bedroom in sight.

Sashaying toward me, each step brought her closer, each stride driving me a little crazier. Till she stood in front of me and snaked her arms around the back of my neck, tugging on my hair to pull my mouth down over hers. I took her into my arms, deepening the kiss, enjoying the way her body molded against mine.

Mine, she was all mine. I let out a long slow sigh.

Then, only frenzied action. I pulled her T-shirt over her head. She unhooked her bra. My hands on her breasts. Man, those fabulous boobs drove me wild.

She ripped off my shirt, staring at my tattoos though she didn't say much about them. It wasn't the tattoos I regretted. It was the life I'd led at the time.

I found a condom in my pocket. My pants went down,

her skirt up. I pressed her up against the door.

Ginger was panting, her hair mussed up, skin glowing, her breaths coming faster. A shrill cry escaped her lips. It tipped me over the edge, excruciating pleasure radiating from my groin. My legs turning to jelly, I could barely stand, stayed pressed up against her for a bit, waiting till I'd caught my breath. Problem was, with this woman, I was never going to be able to keep up.

She nudged me away. "I need some air."

I gave her some space, pulled myself together, pulled my pants back up while I was at it. Ginger wriggled her skirt down to cover herself, looking around for her T-shirt. I reached across and picked it up.

She held her hand out.

I snatched it back. "Not so fast."

"I give up." She moaned and slid down to the floor in a heap, the most beautiful heap I'd ever seen.

I slid right down beside her. "No need to put your T-shirt so soon. You look good that way."

I took one breast into my hand, then stopped to put my arm around her and pulled her in close.

"You don't think they're small?" she asked.

"I think they're perfect."

Leaning across, I teased her nipple with my tongue, then took it into my mouth.

She gasped. "Not so soon."

"You need a rest?" I sat up, shook the hair back from my face. "Shame we're not in bed, then."

"Who needs a bed?"

I pulled her closer and breathed her in, no perfume, no fake fragrances, just my Ginger. If only we could stay like this forever.

I had everything I wanted right here in my arms, but maybe I shouldn't want what I couldn't have. Maybe I shouldn't drag her down.

Because forever wasn't going to happen, not for me.

CHAPTER SIX

Ginger

I couldn't believe Cooper wanted to come with me on this particular job to Wilson High, his old school to be precise. Because no way would I go back to my old school. Ever.

I photographed schools from time to time so they had images for their websites and for other promotional purposes. Still, there was always something strange about walking down a locker-lined hallway when the students were in class because in my memories, the hallways were always bustling and loud with a bit of shoving and pushing. Not now.

Ahead of us, two students turned a corner and stopped in the middle of the hall, their eyes wide, mouths open.

"Oh my God, that's Cooper McVeigh," one of them said.

I stopped, sidling closer to Cooper. "I thought you said they'd never recognize the drummer."

"Um, yeah," he mumbled.

One guy started groping his pockets. "We've *got* to get a photo." Then to Cooper. "Please, please, is that okay?"

"Sure." He set down the handcart loaded with my

equipment. "But we need to make it quick."

He got into position between the two guys, who couldn't stop beaming, one of them stretching his arm out for the selfie.

"Here, let me help." I took the phone from him, snapped a couple of shots, and handed the phone back.

After saying thank you a dozen or so times, the two boys left.

"Sorry, Cooper, but this isn't going to work if the kids keep recognizing you," I said. "It's too disruptive."

"My disguise." He whipped the baseball cap from his back pocket and pulled it over his head. "Besides, the principal won't kick me out."

"No, but *I* might."

I was supposed to be working. He wheeled the handcart while I held onto the tripod. Catherine, the principal, had left us to finish off shots at the library while she went to take an important call, telling us to meet her outside when we were done.

Cooper led the way down the hallway. A guy with scruffy hair and an A$AP Rocky T-shirt sat slumped against the lockers fiddling with the rips on his jeans.

"Got kicked out, eh?" Cooper asked.

The kid smiled, uncomfortable but friendly. "Yeah."

After we passed him, Cooper said, "That used to be me."

"Sorry?"

"I was always acting up in class. Didn't like being told what to do. I had what they call a problem with authority figures. I would much rather have been hanging out with friends."

I stopped by a door at the end of the hall. "Wouldn't

we all?"

Cooper rested his hand on the door, ready to push it open. "Wilson High has good memories for me because this is where I met Nick and Lachie. It's also bad because it reminds me what a dick I was." He tilted his head. "I bet you were an excellent student."

"I guess so."

"And very obedient."

I fluttered my eyelashes. "Yes, I was a good little Korean girl, doing all the right things, ticking all the boxes. It was later on when I got a job at a photographer's studio that I really rocked the boat. Because that wasn't a proper job for someone who should've been at college."

"Your parents didn't approve?"

I shook my head slowly. "They counseled me against photography, found other suitable college courses, even said they could get me a job at my dad's accounting office."

"Wow. But they let you set up your studio in their garage?"

"Begrudgingly. They'd given up on me by then." I motioned toward the door. "We need to get a move on."

"Sure."

Cooper led the way to a shaded courtyard where Catherine was waiting with half a dozen students sitting around on benches, a couple on a table. One of the boys tossed his head back, his laughter floating through the air.

So young, so alive.

Clean cut, dark hair, stunning blue eyes. I glanced at him and saw Mitch. His face flashed in my mind, the last time I'd seen him. Pain gripped my chest, clawing away inside me. How could it hurt so much after all this time?

But it wasn't Mitch. I turned away.

Cooper reached for my shoulder. "Are you okay?"

"Yeah, one of those kids…" I took a deep breath. "He reminded me of someone, that's all."

His hand under my chin, Cooper tipped my head up. "You've gone pale. You're not okay."

I opened my mouth to argue, changed my mind. "No, but I will be."

"Perfect timing," Catherine called out for us to join them.

Stepping closer, I pulled myself together. "You kids look great as you are. Just talk among yourselves while I set up."

I forced myself to concentrate on the task at hand, using available light and a reflector held by my trusty camera assistant. Cooper gave me strength, just by being there, by living and breathing.

The ache in my chest eased. Turned out the young man was nothing like Mitch at all with the possible exception of that laugh and those blue eyes. And I was strong enough to get through this.

The teenagers and their banter brought me back down to earth, reminding me why I liked these jobs so much. Because these kids were so natural with each other, so honest, so young and they had their whole lives ahead of them. It filled me with hope. We all needed a little hope.

After we'd taken a range of shots, one of the girls stared at Cooper. "I know who you are."

He spread his arms. "So do I."

"You're Cooper McVeigh."

Followed by raised voices and lots of ooh and ahs.

"Catherine," I said. "I can explain—"

She shook her head. "It's okay. I know. Cooper called me about this yesterday."

"He did?"

What on earth was going on? I stared at Cooper, but he was too busy trying to control the kids who were asking him questions, talking one on top of the other.

"Hold it, guys." He held his hands out, waiting for some quiet. "I heard one of you asking about the drug scene."

A boy nodded. "Yeah, me. Aren't you some sort of stoner?"

"Maybe I was at school but that was a long time ago." His expression serious, Cooper slowed down. "I also used to hang out with Nick Steel and Lachie Tyler too, both of them very successful, something that would never have happened if they'd been stoned off their faces all the time."

"You're just saying that." The kid wouldn't give up. "I bet you smoked a ton of dope. I read about it."

Cooper turned to Catherine. "Can I speak frankly?"

She nodded. "You may."

"I've seen what drugs do to people." Cooper paused, pain in his eyes. "I had another friend, an older guy who was a brilliant guitarist, and I watched him die from hepatitis. His liver gave way, skin turned yellow, a long slow death." Cooper paced from side to side. "I'm telling it like it is. You're a dick if you do drugs."

If Cooper was being too blunt for the school principal, she wasn't letting it show. The kids stayed still, their eyes wide and riveted to Cooper.

"Whoa," one of them said.

The other kids may have been speechless but the

principal wasn't. "Come on, you should all get to class."

After they left, Catherine turned to Cooper. "I know this isn't quite what you had in mind, but would you like to come back and talk to a larger group of students?"

He nodded. "Sure."

"Because they need to hear a strong drugs message from someone who's been there, someone they admire, someone a lot cooler than any of their teachers. It'd mean so much for them to get this from the horse's mouth, so to speak."

Cooper grinned. "No problem, I'll be the horse."

Catherine laughed, looked more relaxed than she had all day. "We can talk about some of your other ideas another time."

What other ideas did she mean and what had they been talking about? This was a side to Cooper I hadn't seen before, but it didn't surprise me, not too much.

"Is there anything else you need photographed?" I asked Catherine.

"Let's call it a day." She looked me in the eye. "I'm very happy with the way this went. Hope you don't mind but I've got a meeting lined up now."

She left, while I got back to packing up my equipment. Sometimes it seemed a never-ending task—set up, pack away, next location.

I crouched down to put my camera in its bag. "I'm starving."

"I can see if there's anything decent from the cafeteria," Cooper said.

"It's worth a try."

"There's a nice, quiet spot on the grass out in front of the school."

"Sure, we can pretend it's a picnic."

He took my hand. "Let's get going."

Cooper had it all planned out, walking with me along a path at the front of the school that led to a sunny grassed area with a lovely view through a copse of trees to the road.

I waited with my gear while Cooper came back with sandwiches from the cafeteria. The view only got better with his return. Sitting opposite me, he passed across a sandwich and a bottle of water.

I took a bite and chewed. "Not so bad. So do you want to tell me what it is you're going to talk about with Catherine? You two seemed very chummy back there."

"I wouldn't say we're 'friends' exactly. I'm tossing around a few ideas, that's all. At first I was thinking of some sort of scholarship for underprivileged teens or kids who deserve it. Now I think that might work better if I speak to someone from Frankston University, I'm not really sure."

"Wow, they're big ideas."

"Bigger than me, hopefully. That's the point."

"You didn't mention anything earlier."

Already halfway through his sandwich, he gulped back some water. "Because I haven't decided exactly what to do."

"It's very generous of you."

"Not really. I just don't want to mess things up again. There's a big difference."

I kept eating, didn't say anything.

Cooper raised his eyebrows. "You seem to think I'm a good person?"

"Well, yeah." It seemed such a dumb question.

"I'm not nearly as nice as you think I am, Ginger. I'm better than I used to be, but not good, not by a long shot. If you'd met me a few years ago, you'd think I was a complete jerk."

"Are we back to this again?" I asked. "You're not like that now."

"I'm not done yet. You need to hear this."

My gaze hardened. "No, I don't."

Still, I didn't move away, couldn't bring myself to.

Cooper sighed. "I never got into heavy drugs, just smoked a bit of dope and drank. A lot. Never really got addicted to anything, not in a way that I could never give it up. But I chose to keep going the way I was. My problem wasn't addiction. It was that I was an asshole."

So that was why he didn't drink. I let his words sink in.

"Then, a few years ago, everything changed," he said. "A car crash. I was pissed out of my brain and ended up wrapping the car around a lamppost. I was lucky to get out alive. My fault, my actions, my responsibility. It took lying in a hospital bed for weeks on end with my back in a brace for me to come to my senses."

I nodded. I'd read about the crash and how it was a life-changing moment.

He lowered his gaze. "I didn't want to end up dead at twenty-seven like Amy Winehouse or Kurt Cobain. And I didn't want to end up like the guy from Motley Crue who was driving drunk and ended up killing his best friend. I didn't want that to be me, so I had to change."

"You have changed. The person you're describing isn't the guy sitting in front of me."

"I've altered the bits on the outside and I'm trying to be a good person, truly I am, but that's not what's inside me. I can't be the guy you want me to be."

"I want you to be you." Frustration simmered inside me because I wasn't getting through. "And so far, I like what I've seen."

He shook his head. "It's better you know the sort of person I am before you get too involved with me."

My stomach dropped. *Before* I got too involved? When was before? The attraction, the involvement, the relationship had been instant. No waiting, no thinking, no considering the consequences.

Because this was life. Life wasn't for waiting around or ticking things off lists. It was for living. Mitch's short life had taught me that. We had to live and love today because that was all we had.

My lips thinned. "Don't tell me you're not involved. Don't even think about it."

"I'm just saying we should try and keep things light. One way or another, I'll end up hurting you, Ginger, and I don't want that to happen."

I stood, brushed the grass from the back of my pants. "I'm already involved."

He scrambled to his feet. "I'm sorry."

"Don't be sorry. Just don't be an asshole. For crying out loud, Cooper, you're the one who wanted to come along on the shoot today, remember? The one who came to the studio, who was happy to meet my mom. And you're not exactly holding back when it comes to having sex. You've never given any indication you wanted to go slow. And now you come out with this crap."

He pushed back his hair. "This has come out all wrong. Can we forget I said anything?"

"No, we can't forget everything and go back in time.

We can only go forward."

He drew me into his arms and held me close, my reservations dissolving in his embrace. I should be stronger. Stand up for myself. Push him away.

Mom had told me he wasn't the marrying kind. Now he was telling me himself. But I wasn't hounding him for a marriage proposal.

I just wanted a piece of him, and I wanted to give myself to him. Was that too much to ask?

CHAPTER SEVEN

Cooper

Our first argument, followed by make-up sex. Whatever we did, it seemed to be followed by sex and I wasn't complaining about that part. I'd made it up to Ginger over the last week, not with grand gestures and statements, but by spending time together. If only we had more time.

I didn't know how she did it. Sitting at the table beside me, Ginger made a fitted black lace top with a floaty burgundy skirt look the right balance of elegant and casual for any venue.

She glanced around the restaurant. "I wasn't sure if you'd select some expensive, fine dining place."

I'd chosen Domenic's, an old family favorite with wood paneling and red checkered tablecloths, a restaurant where big servings won over presentation. No fancy places for my parents, and this dinner was for them.

I placed a hand on my chest. "Me? Do I look like a guy who's interested in Michelin stars?"

Ginger gave me a teasing smile. "I'm surprised you know what they are."

Clearing my throat, I looked across at my mom. "I

haven't given you your present yet."

"But you got us the champagne," she said.

"That was from Ginger."

"Oh, I didn't realize." Mom turned to her. "That's so kind. You didn't need to bring anything."

I laughed. "That's what I told her."

My parents always insisted their wedding anniversary wasn't necessarily a communal celebration, but I'd been a shitty son in the past and was making up for the birthdays I'd missed and the Christmas when I hadn't bothered calling. I had a lot to make up for.

"It was my pleasure," Ginger said. "Also my favorite champagne so I hope you enjoy it."

"We certainly will." Dad leaned forward. "I like to think of myself as being very well rounded. I can enjoy everything from Pabst to Piper-Heidsieck."

"How open-minded of you," I said.

Dad's eyes narrowed. "No need to be cheeky."

"Hey." I pointed a finger. "If you're not good, I won't give you your present."

I asked Ginger for the envelope which I'd left in her purse. She dug out her camera at the same time, a small Lumix she used when she didn't want to lug around her huge Canon outfit.

I handed the envelope to Mom. "I'll give this to the responsible adult."

As she opened it and looked at the card, that warm-and-fuzzy-mom expression came over her face, followed by incredulity as she examined the printouts I'd included—one each for their air tickets, one for accommodation in Zurich and Amsterdam, and one for the cruise along the Rhine.

Her mouth open, she showed the pages to Dad who was equally open-mouthed.

"How did you know?" she spluttered.

I'd had the conversation with her years ago about the bucket list and things she wanted to see and do. This cruise was her number one. And now she had it. God knew she deserved more than I could give after all the crap I'd put the two of them through.

"Thank you so much." Mom nearly knocked her chair back as she came over to give me a hug. I stood and hugged her right back.

Ginger lifted her camera and took a couple of shots because she liked to capture everyday moments, even if this wasn't exactly an everyday sort of gift.

While Mom was sitting down and composing herself, Dad came over for a bear hug. A big bear of a man himself, he'd never been one to show affection in public until a couple of years ago when everything had changed. At least one good thing had come from all of that.

We all took our seats while Ginger sat there beaming. Happy, just the way I liked her. My folks thanked me over and over again.

Dad leaned back in his chair. "I'll have to check out all those German beers while we're traveling."

"And the Heineken in Amsterdam," I added.

Mom stared at Dad. "And the scenery and culture, the castles along the Rhine, the historic towns and cities."

"Of course." He looked at me and I'd be damned if his lower lip wasn't quivering. "It's very generous of you, son."

"No need to be so serious." I picked up my glass of mineral water. "Happy anniversary."

"Cooper is very kind and considerate." Ginger raised her eyebrows. "Problem is, he doesn't want anyone to know."

"Not true," I protested.

She told them how I was exploring ways I could help students with some sort of scholarship. Hell, I hadn't even worked out the best way of doing things or how I was going handle that. I only knew I wanted to leave a piece of me behind, not a legacy, not exactly because that was too corny. It simply seemed that I had enough money and I'd done enough selfish shit in my lifetime that it wouldn't hurt to do some small good in the world.

I turned to her. "Anyway, you're a much better person than me."

"Not really, and the fact I looked after my brother barely counts."

"Sorry?" I had a feeling I'd missed something.

"Oh, it was ages ago." She frowned. "I must've told you about Alistair's illness."

"N-no, you haven't," I said.

She sucked in a slow breath. "When Alistair was twelve, he got cancer. Went through surgery, chemo, the works."

What a shock. "Ginger, I had no idea."

"I'm so sorry to hear that," Mom said, pain glimmering in her eyes because she knew what it was like to have a sick child.

"So what about Alistair?" I asked.

"I helped feed him and played with him and generally tried to take his mind off things," Ginger said. "Mom talks about me being his savior but it wasn't like that. He needed a hand, and I helped, end of story. And he got better. Like I said, it was a long time ago."

Ginger shrugged as if it were nothing but it was far from that. This woman was truly something.

I held her gaze. "I didn't think there was an expiration date on kindness."

She laughed it off, sidling closer to me. "Forget about that."

"Some things are hard to forget."

"No, please don't argue when I'm trying to change the subject. I had a great idea. We should go on our own vacation. Not to Europe. That's too far." She paused. "To the desert."

Where the hell had that come from? "The desert?"

"Yeah, it's so beautiful."

"It is?"

She gave me a gentle whack. "I definitely have to take you out there so you can see how stunning it is. It's beautiful at dawn."

"I don't do dawn. That's way too early for me."

Something shifted inside me. She had no way of knowing how hard this would be for me, how near impossible.

"Then, sunset," she said. "The cactus in flower, the sandstone cliffs and red rocks, the rawness of the landscape... I can't believe you grew up in Frankston and you've never been to the desert."

"We've been," Dad said. "But he always got bored in the back of the car with his sister."

Amy and I had both found it torturous but she wasn't here to stick up for me about how dull that had been. She was tagging along with her husband at some business conference in D.C.

Ginger tugged at my arm. "We should do it. A couple of nights in the desert, just me and you. I've got a tent and all the gear. And I can take photos. That's what I usually do."

My gut clenched. It sounded so romantic and I'd love to be stuck in the desert with her. I'd love to be stuck anywhere with her, but I couldn't be so far from civilization for any length of time. Not for two nights, not even one.

"Come on." She went all doe eyed. "I've never believed any of that stuff people say about how Frankston is like nineties Seattle in the middle of nowhere. The desert isn't nowhere. We're surrounded by beauty, only most people don't see it."

"I'm certainly surrounded by beauty." I spread my arms. "I've got you on one side and my mom on the other, the two most beautiful women in the world."

Dad took Mom's hand into his. "I second that."

Ginger pouted, her eyes narrowing as she held my gaze. "You won't go to the desert because you think it'll be ugly and boring. You have to come. You have to."

I got up. "Actually I have to go to the bathroom."

I had to change the subject, change her mind, change everything, and get out of here because I couldn't deal with this now.

Dad was waiting for me in the hallway outside the bathroom at the back of the restaurant when I came out. Arms folded, deep lines bracketed his mouth, lines I'd put there.

I stopped in front of him, dread filling my gut as I waited for the words I knew would be coming.

"You should tell her, son," he said.

"I know." My chest tightened. "I will. Not tonight, though."

I turned to leave but Dad gave me another of those hugs, then headed straight for the bathroom before I could see the tears in his eyes. He might as well have yanked my heart out of my chest right there and then.

I couldn't get enough air, couldn't breathe. I thought about Dave dying of hepatitis, ashamed he could have been so stupid as to share needles, devastated at what it was doing to his family, so rundown he couldn't play guitar, so sick he didn't want to go on anymore.

Not now. I had to get my shit together and quickly.

Taking deep breaths, I forced myself to stand up straight and stride around the corner toward the table where my two favorite women were waiting because tonight was for celebrating.

Ginger looked up at me as I sat down beside her. "Grandmother's birthday is coming up. I was just telling your mom how it's a big thing. We have a huge feast."

I'd never been so grateful for normal conversation— normal, the thing I longed for.

"Great," I said.

"Mom told my gran about you so I'm stuck. You have to come, and you have to eat a lot. That's how these things work."

"Sounds good. Count me in."

I forced a smile to my face. It reminded me how we should make the most of all our time with the people we love.

Dad came back and we had more of that normal conversation. Mom and Ginger shared a tiramisu for dessert while Dad had another beer, which he said was better than any of the desserts on the menu. At least he knew what he wanted.

There was more hugging at the end of the evening before we left the restaurant, then Mom and Dad went one way and we went the other.

Ginger stumbled so I put my arm around her.

"Ooh, I might've had more to drink than I thought," she said.

"Not that much."

"The last glass may have tipped me over the edge. What can I say? I'm a cheap drunk."

"Not with your taste in champagne!"

She pretended to be outraged as we got into the car.

"You look so funny when you're angry." I started the car, then held her gaze. "I wish I'd known you when you were a teenager. I bet you were cute."

"Hey, I'm still cute."

I walked my fingers along her thigh. "I could've seen how long it took to get to first base." I nuzzled into her neck. "We could've made out in the back row of the cinema or maybe I'd have taken you to the lake."

"The lake? No guy ever took me there."

"Are you serious?"

My eyes widened. "Not even when you were in high school?"

"Nope. I'm not saying I never made out with any guys at school." Indignation in her voice. "Only that I've never been taken to the lake."

"Well, all that's about to change." I put on the turn signal and took a right. "I haven't been here for years."

After a short drive, I pulled into the parking lot and walked around to open the car door for Ginger. There were a couple of other cars in the lot, but no people to be seen. She slid off her sandals so I took off my shoes too, and slid my hand into hers.

The stillness of the night air enveloped us as we wandered closer to the lake, the soft crunch of grass underfoot the only sound to be heard. I led her further along and we settled under a tree, far from the lights of the parking lot.

She lay down on the grass while I stared across at the lake, the crescent moon a tiny reflection on its surface. I reminded myself that I had Ginger and we had this time together.

"It's not exactly Tahoe," I said.

"I've never been there," Ginger mumbled.

"I can take you." I lay down beside her, trailing my fingers along her arm. "I can take you anywhere you want."

She giggled. "A come on line, if I've ever heard one."

I pressed little kisses to her neck, my hand on her waist. "I heard this was your first time."

Snaking her arm around my neck, she pulled my mouth down over hers. She tasted like white wine, my dessert, right here beside me. I deepened the kiss. If all I had was this moment, our two bodies intertwined on the grass, tongues rolling, breath deepening, then things wouldn't be so bad at all.

My hand inched higher up over her top till I covered her breast with my hand, kneading the soft flesh. I kept going, could've stayed that way all night.

Ginger broke off the kiss, pushed me onto my side so we were facing each other.

She smiled. "Guess you made it to first base."

"Oh, was that first base?" I drew her closer into another kiss, one hand sliding up her back under her top till I unfastened her bra and slid my hand right back where it'd been before, onto the bare skin of her breast this time. She let out a little moan. I kept going. "See, I thought *this* was first base."

She pushed me away and laughed, such a beautiful sound.

"You know what the problem is," she said. "You've got too many clothes on."

She undid the buttons of my shirt one by one and slid it off my shoulders, the cool night air prickling my skin. I covered her mouth with mine, our tongues rolling against each other till I needed to stop for air.

"And I thought you weren't the sort of girl who kissed on the first date," I whispered.

She giggled. I pulled up her skirt, sliding my hand along her slender thigh. The giggling stopped. Settling between her legs, I edged her panties down slowly, made her wait.

I went down on her, kissed her the way I wanted to, fast, slow, gentle, hard, calm, intense. This was for Ginger. I kept going till she let out a shrill cry, her body going from tense to relaxed in an instant. Just what I'd wanted.

Now we were done, I pulled her skirt down loosely over her thighs because I was one hell of a gentleman, and lay down beside her.

Seconds later, muffled voices cut through the air, footsteps traipsing through the grass, followed by giggling, the sort that came from teenage girls.

Ginger stiffened, grabbed me. I sat up, pulling her up beside me. Six slim silhouettes passed in front of us, kept their distance, just teenagers passing by. One of them chugged back some beer and threw the empty can aside as they walked. More muffled voices.

"Wow, aren't they a bit old for that?" The voice was tinged with disgust.

Ginger covered her mouth, her body shaking as she held back her laughter till they'd passed.

"We were so busted," she said.

"I know. By a bunch of teenagers. It should've been the other way around."

"Who the hell cares?" She relaxed back on her elbows, her eyes glinting in the dim light as she curled her index finger for me to join her. "We're not done yet."

That was the problem. I was never going to be done with Ginger. Sex wasn't enough. I had to have all of her.

Giving up booze hadn't been easy but I'd been determined because there'd been so much at stake. So different from now. I'd tried pushing her away but couldn't let go. I was like a drug addict, desperate for one more day together, one more hit.

And no matter how much I got, it was never enough. I could never have too much of this woman.

Damn it, I should've stuck with what I'd known. Kept things shallow. Not got too involved. Only now it was too late to turn back.

CHAPTER EIGHT

Ginger

I was never going to understand this guy. How could Cooper say he wasn't a good person when he was here at Frankston General doing something so kind and generous?

Lachie had clearly been here and done this many times before. The nursing staff knew him and seemed thrilled to meet Cooper, even if he was only the drummer. His words, not mine, because there was no 'only' where Cooper was concerned.

I'd been to the adolescent ward often enough when I was a kid so it seemed familiar and strange at the same time. It made me wonder if I'd blocked out some of the memories. I certainly couldn't remember the lime counter and purple wall at reception. That had to be new.

We wandered out of one room into the corridor, ready to go to the next ward.

Cooper reached for Lachie's arm. "Hey, I'm not trying to step on your toes."

"No problem, man. I was hardly going to say you couldn't come."

"Yeah, but I didn't want to be like the third wheel."

I held up my hand. "No, that would be me."

Lachie smiled. "No way. Any friend of Cooper's is a friend of mine." He looked around. "Let's get moving. Only two more rooms to go."

We'd already been to the girls' ward and most of the boys' section, giving away caps and CDs from the bags in our hands. I helped by carrying a bag but left it up to the boys to hand the stuff out.

Cooper and I exchanged a loving glance. He could make me feel special, no matter the place or time.

Meanwhile Lachie led the way. A seasoned pro, he introduced himself and Cooper as he walked in.

The boy in the closest bed sat up ram rod straight. "Oh my God, you're from The Merchants."

Lachie spoke to him while Cooper made his way to the next bed to a kid who looked about fourteen, his mouth hanging open.

"I take it you've heard of us?" Cooper said.

He grinned. "Have I ever!"

I glanced at the bed chart. Non-Hodgkin's lymphoma, the same type of cancer as Alistair. My throat tightened. I had a pretty good idea what the poor kid was going through, the treatments, the hospital stays, the nausea, the pain.

As I wandered closer to Cooper, he gave my hand a quick squeeze without turning around. As if he could sense my anticipation.

"So what do you do when you're not hanging around hospital rooms?" he asked the kid.

"I play football mostly but I'm into all kinds of sports." The boy's eyes widened. "Meeting you makes me want to become a musician instead of a football player."

"A lot of people would argue that drummers aren't musicians," Cooper quipped.

"What?"

Cooper shrugged. "An old drummer joke, no big deal."

"It's *so* not true. You're a great drummer and you guys are my favorite band." The kid motioned for Cooper to come closer. "I've got a girlfriend and we made out to *Always at Midnight*. That song really helped—" he nudged Cooper —"if you know what I mean."

Cooper laughed. "Oh, I do."

Football player, all-round sportsman, and a ladies' man, this kid cracked me up. I pulled a T-shirt out of the bag in my hand. Only one left. Cooper held my gaze for a moment then took the shirt and handed it to the boy, who whooped with appreciation.

"It's a bit big but it's fantastic. Wow, thanks so much." He reached up to give Cooper a one-armed hug while keeping his other hand secured around the tee.

"You'll grow into it, my man," Cooper said.

He would. He'd grow older and taller and live a long, happy life. Like Alistair. At least I hoped he would. My heart surged with hope, held back by vulnerability. At times like this, the frailty of human life hit home.

When I'd been ten and Alistair twelve, going in and out of the hospital all the time, I hadn't thought that way. Though I'd overheard my parents talking and seen with my own eyes how sick Alistair had become, I'd refused to believe he wouldn't make it. He was my brother and, as far as I'd been concerned, he was always going to be there.

I knew better now, of course, and understood exactly how serious his condition had been. *Touch and go*, that was what the doctors had said at one point. I shuddered just thinking about it.

Cooper went on to talk to the next kid, Lachie too, making their way around the room.

I'd never visited Mitch in the hospital because he'd never made it that far. I didn't even know how to remember him because the last time I'd seen him, we'd argued. A horrible memory. He'd held his ground and I'd cried my guts out, my heart breaking and my life falling apart.

The next time I saw him was in an open casket. So young. Such a tragedy. That wasn't how I wanted to remember him either. I'd leaned over and kissed him on the cheek while his mom sobbed silently beside me. Then I'd lost it completely and the guy from the funeral home had taken my hand and led me away.

I blinked back the tears. That was years ago and I was never going there again.

Cooper looked across at me and came over. "Are you okay?"

"Sure, fine."

Out in the corridor, Lachie stopped. "Hey, I just realized, you didn't bring your camera."

"No, it didn't feel right," I said. "If you're doing something good, then that should be enough in itself without making a big deal of it."

He nodded. "I gotta agree."

"Isn't there another room to go?" I asked.

Lachie stiffened. "I'm okay. It's just... There was this one kid, Brandon, who used to be in the last room right here. I barely knew him but, you know, sometimes you make a connection. And it's as if I keep expecting to see him." A pause. "He didn't make it."

My heart sank. "I'm sorry."

Cooper put his hand on Lachie's shoulder, making me think Lachie's pain ran deep.

"My dad has bowel cancer," he said. "He had a bad run but he's in remission now. He's one of the lucky ones."

Poor Lachie. He and his family had clearly been through the wringers. No one deserved that.

I nodded. "Yeah, it's lucky we're all healthy."

Lachie and Cooper's face turned ashen, neither of them saying a word, silence hanging over us like a shroud. Had I said something wrong? Was there something I didn't know about?

Then we went into the room for a final round of greetings and Oh My Gods while the guys did their thing.

Back in the corridor again, Lachie gave me a quick kiss on the cheek and shook Cooper's hand.

"I've gotta go," he said.

As he was striding away from us, I turned to Cooper. "You've never been here before, have you?"

"No, I said I hadn't."

"So why come here today with Lachie?"

Holding my gaze, his eyes narrowed, expression intense. We stayed like that for a few long moments. The hair on the back of my neck prickled, my senses alert. I might not know exactly what was going on but I knew when something was off.

He grabbed my arm. "We need to talk. Let's go back to your place."

I pulled my arm back. "What's going on?"

"I can't talk about this here. Your place, Ginger.

Now."

"Fine."

I marched ahead of him in a way that said this was absolutely not fine. In fact, I had a horrible feeling nothing would be fine again. How come Lachie seemed to know what was going on when I didn't? And why was this conversation suddenly urgent?

The walk to the parking lot took an eternity, the drive home even longer, our silence a wall between us. The quiet when he pulled up in the parking lot at the rear of my building nearly killed me. No car engine, no noise from the street, no kids playing on the grass. Nothing.

Cooper slipped out of the car in a flash, opening my door for me before I had a chance to get my act together.

"No need to play the gentleman," I muttered under my breath.

He placed his hands on my shoulders, his breath warm on the back of my neck. "This isn't a game, Ginger."

My heart racing, I took a long slow breath. He was pissing me off and I didn't care if I showed it. Maybe that wasn't good enough and I should be a bit more mature about this. I pulled my shoulders back, turned to face him, and took his hands into mine, then nodded toward the steps that led to my apartment.

Inside, I tossed my purse onto a chair in the living room and sat on the sofa.

"I'm sorry." I dropped my head into my hands. "It's just that I'm getting a little tired of the cool and mysterious routine."

Cooper slid beside me onto the sofa, close but not too close. Was he breaking up with me? Was that what this was all about?

He looked down at his hands. "There's something I haven't told you and there's no nice way of saying this, Ginger. I'm sick."

I didn't understand. "Of me?"

"No, never." Still, he didn't look at me. "Two years ago, I went to the doctor for a regular checkup. I don't even know why I went because I felt fine. It was one of those things. Almost as if subconsciously I knew."

"Knew what?"

"The doctor did a blood test, a liver biopsy, a bunch of other tests because he picked something up right away and there were several possibilities. Turned out it was the worst possible scenario." He looked across at me. "I've got autoimmune hepatitis."

Hepatitis? Surely he couldn't be talking about drugs and sharing needles. Getting legless drunk—that was something I could picture Cooper doing even though I'd never seen him drink—but sticking a needle into his arm was a whole different ballgame. Shit, what had happened?

He held a hand out. "First of all, I'm not contagious. You can't get the disease through having sex or anything like that."

I should be relieved. Instead, I stiffened, my gut clenching.

"I know what you're thinking," he said. "I did a lot of dumb, selfish things but I never did intravenous. And none of those stupid things I did helped bring this on. AIH has nothing to do with drugs or drinking or promiscuity. That's another word doctors love to use. They think there's a genetic predisposition but they're not really sure. There's no known cause."

"AIH?"

So he was practically on first name terms with this disease. Something clawed away inside me, a desperate desire to make things right, a need to know more.

"Your body's immune system turns against liver cells and the liver gets inflamed," he said. "You need your liver. It's a vital organ."

He was sick. I got that. But it sounded like the disease had been diagnosed early, and there were treatments. There had to be. I thought about everything Alistair had been through. I'd been there with him and I'd be there with Cooper.

My heart twisted, every nerve in my body on edge for all the wrong reasons. I'd stay by his side, give him hugs when he needed them, drive him to doctors' appointments, stay by his side when he was ill. Whatever it took, we'd get through this.

He'd need me to be strong. I cleared my throat to keep the falter from my voice.

Sliding closer, I put my arm around him. "I'm so sorry, Cooper. I would never have guessed." There'd been some weird stuff but nothing that would have led me here. "You don't *look* sick."

"I don't feel sick most of the time either. Just really, really tired. It's not a normal 'tired' either. It's my body telling me something's wrong. I've had some nausea, joint pain, nothing too serious yet. But it'll get bad. Real bad."

I swallowed the lump in my throat. It'd get worse. Then it'd get better. Surely that was what he meant.

"What are the treatments? Is there any medication that helps?"

He nodded. "I take loads of drugs, all of them prescribed. They suppress the immune system, and they help. To a degree."

"Well, that's good."

He covered his mouth with one hand, then let it drop. "This isn't hep C. People with hep C often live a long time."

A muscle in Cooper's jaw flinched, his expression hardening. The sparkling blue eyes that had only ever been warm and loving lost their vitality.

"It's not good, Ginger. There's no cure for autoimmune hepatitis."

No, he had this wrong. There was something the doctors could do. There had to be.

A picture of Mitch's pale face in the open casket flashed in my mind. Dear God, not again. I couldn't go there, couldn't breathe. How would I be able to breathe without Cooper? My pulse was racing so fast I couldn't catch up.

"What do you mean there's no cure?"

"I'm terminal. That's what I'm trying to tell you."

Just like that, my heart was yanked from my chest and my world shattered into a thousand pieces.

CHAPTER NINE

Cooper

The color drained from Ginger's face, a strange guttural sound escaping her lips, a moan from deep within.

I pulled her closer, drawing her into a hug because I needed one as much as she did.

"Cooper," she mumbled.

Drained, she pushed her limp arms around me while I did all the hugging. The poor thing had no energy. Hardly surprising when this was the first time for her, whereas I'd been through this before.

Not that I was used to it. Some things, you never get used to.

Tears streamed down her face. "Tell me this is some sort of cruel joke. Anything, anything but this."

I held her gaze, looked at what I'd done to her, and shook my head. My heart ached from the pain I was causing, my chest tight.

She grabbed my arm, dug her fingernails into my skin. "How can you be terminal?"

"I'm sorry, Ginger. For everything." I pulled myself together quick smart to keep the quaver from my voice. I was absolutely not going to lose my shit when I'd given this news to the woman I loved.

"And you? What about you, Cooper? How can you be … dying?"

"The prognosis is for five to ten years."

I knew the statistics: a survival rate of fifty percent at five years, ten percent at ten years. Statistics didn't mean shit when you were the one who had the incurable disease. The only statistic that was a certainty was that I'd get cirrhosis and die. That was one thing the doctors had been clear about—when I developed cirrhosis, my time was even more limited.

Stick to the facts, Cooper. I forced myself to stay even.

"You're twenty-five." Ginger's voice cracked. "Ten years. Oh my God, thirty-five is still so young."

I took a moment, wasn't sure how much bad news she could take all at once. "I've already had AIH for two years."

She slapped a hand over her mouth, then let it drop, realization dawning in her eyes. "That's why you don't drink."

I nodded. "Not a single drop since I found out. Drinking is one of the worst things I could do and I figured, hey, I'd probably drunk enough before then anyway. That part's not so bad. I'd already cleaned up my act after the car crash."

"So why? Why you?"

"There's no reason, no good answer. That's the irony of it. Nothing bad happened to me when I was being a drunken asshole, except for the crash, and even that turned out to be a good thing because it was an awakening. It was only after I was living the life of a saint—by rock standards anyway—that I got this disease."

I sucked in a deep breath. Better to get this all off my chest now, while I could still speak, before I fell apart or clammed up. Because most of the time, I didn't talk about it, couldn't bear to.

"I'm the reason The Merchants came back to Frankston," I said. "The line we gave to the media and everyone else was that we came back so Lachie could be close to his father during his cancer treatment. We also said we were writing songs and recording the next album. And hanging around for The Salt Flats Festival. All partly true. We weren't exactly lying."

I was also the reason Nick and Lachie had been so pissed off at Austin when he'd said he was leaving the band. Because that was only going to leave the two of them. And two out of four isn't a whole band. I'd tried to tell them Austin had every right, that it was his life to live as he wished and his decision. I knew better than most that we only get one life.

"Soon the guys'll need to find a new drummer," I added. "Recording is one thing. I should be able to help out with that but there's no way they can rely on me to play The Flats. It's too high energy, too many variables, too high risk."

Ginger sobbed. "How can you talk about the band as if that's the only thing that matters?"

Because the band was part of me, and giving up The Merchants was like having a vital internal organ ripped from my rib cage. I needed them to breathe. Now I needed something else. Someone.

I pulled Ginger closer, resting her head against my chest. "I came back to Frankston for a reason. My family. I wanted—more than wanted—*needed* to be close to them."

Her body shook. "Oh, God, your poor parents."

Pain rocketed through my chest at what this was doing to them, the two people who'd raised me and given me everything.

I held Ginger and let her sob, but bit back my own tears. I'd cried so much already and couldn't let her down more than I already had. It'd only be harder for her if I broke down too.

Eventually, I said, "It's why I can't go to the desert with you."

"Why?"

The eternal why. I didn't have all the answers but I had this one.

"I can visit the desert, sure," I said. "But I can't camp out so far from civilization, hours from medical care, because if something goes wrong, it'll go very wrong and I'll need immediate attention."

"We don't have to camp out." Desperation soaked through her voice. "We can just visit. A day trip."

"Sure we can."

After a while, she asked, "Who else knows?"

"My family, the guys in the band. They're like family."

"Joel?"

"No, I haven't told him."

Not yet.

Her hands on my chest, she pressed me away, looking up at me with red-rimmed eyes. "You're so calm, Cooper."

"Only on the outside." My voice cracked. *Honesty, tell it like it is. Get it all out there.* "Truth is, I'm a mess, Ginger. I'm pretending I'm okay because that's my way of getting through it, but I'm not that good of an actor."

"Me neither." She trembled in my arms.

I held her gaze. "You're a terrible actress."

My words brought a wan smile to her face. Her lower lip trembled as she tried to hold herself together. Determination glimmered in her eyes. Trying so hard. And failing. My beautiful Ginger exploded into uncontrollable sobbing, so I folded her into my arms, rubbed her back, kissed the tears from her cheeks.

Another thing that was my fault. My heart seized up. What had I done? How could I have let things come so far between us?

Damn it, I was prepared for the twenty questions and the explanations I had to give. It was everything else I wasn't prepared for.

I should've told her sooner. Should've done everything differently.

Most of all, I should never have fallen in love with her.

"I wish I could tell you everything will be all right," I said.

But I couldn't. So many things that were never going to be right.

She nuzzled into my chest, my shirt already wet with her tears, not that I cared. I held her shaking body close and soothed her as best I could. The only way to do that properly would be to go back in time, perhaps to a time before I'd met her.

But I couldn't bear the thought of never having met her. We'd only known each other a matter of weeks—not long in the scheme of things, not even to someone with my prognosis—yet those weeks meant everything to me.

I reached across for a couple of cushions, placing them at one end of the sofa, then lay down with Ginger in my arms. I couldn't say how long we lay there like that, our bodies intertwined, her heart beating against mine, when her breathing became more rhythmic.

I let her sleep. She needed it. Any other day, we'd have been ripping each other's clothes off and rolling around together. Not today. I could hope that maybe one day things would get back to normal between us, except experience had told me that normal didn't exist anymore.

Eventually her eyes fluttered open, her lips curving to a sad smile as she pressed a little kiss to my cheek.

And for a moment I fooled myself that maybe we could forget, maybe we could go back to the way things were.

I kissed her on the mouth. She kissed me back at first, then edged away.

"What's up?" I asked.

"I might have morning breath."

"It's not morning and you weren't asleep that long."

Cozying up to me, she looked at me with a sleepy gaze, still smiling. If only I could keep that smile on her face. If only I could change everything. If only the dread from my disease didn't weigh so heavily on me.

After a while, she said, "I worked out why you brought me back to my place instead of yours. Because I couldn't walk out and leave."

"Pretty much."

I can't run away either. My heart clenched, pain ripping through my chest, my throat tight. We needed to move on from this or I wouldn't be able to hold it together.

"Might be time for some dinner," I said.

She let out a little moan. "I don't feel like cooking."

I sat up. "I can cook. I'm not completely useless."

"When it comes to the kitchen, you are."

"Hey, them's fighting words."

She stood up, straightening her clothes and pushing her hair back as if she was getting up to help.

"I can do pasta," I said. "*I'm* cooking, remember?"

"Okay, sure."

We wandered to the kitchen together, chatting while I chopped the ingredients for carbonara, and Ginger sat slumped at the table. I only knew how to cook about three dishes. My parents had taught me the basics, but then The Merchants had taken off and my life changed. When we were on the road, the only options were takeout or restaurants, and that had suited me fine. The option where someone else cooked for me had also been appealing even if it was slack on my part.

But it shouldn't be about what other people were doing for me. And I had to admit, cooking was fun when it was for someone else.

Ginger poured mineral water for me, opened a bottle of sauvignon blanc from the fridge and poured herself a glass.

"I hope you don't mind." She sat back down at the table. "But I think I need it."

I placed two bowls of steaming pasta on the table. "No problem."

As we clinked glasses, something surged inside me, desire, need, the memory of how things used to be.

At that moment, I would've killed for a glass of wine.

But I wouldn't die for it.

"Hey, this is excellent." Ginger's eyes widened as she chewed her first mouthful of pasta.

I raised my eyebrows. "So, ah, what was it you were

saying about me being completely useless in the kitchen?"

Head down, she kept eating. "Nothing."

She asked a couple more questions about autoimmune hepatitis and what the doctors had said. I answered them. She asked about my parents and sister and the guys in the band, perhaps because she was searching for what was a normal reaction or maybe just because she cared about them.

I could cope if I didn't talk too much about myself. God knows I'd already been through the various stages of grief, first of all denial and anger. I hadn't bothered much with bargaining because I'd already cleaned up my act so there was nothing left to barter with. Which had only pissed me off even more, made me feel more alone, deepened my depression till I'd sunk into the pits of despair.

And now just that one final stage to go through.

I ignored the anguish gripping my chest, forced myself to be a better person and to think of Ginger because that was where my heart lay.

Reaching across the table, I covered her hand with mine. "I don't want this to consume us. I don't want everything we do to be about me and my illness."

"No." She straightened. "I'd like to be clear about something too. Just because you're sick doesn't mean you can back out on me, Cooper McVeigh. I still need a camera assistant from time to time."

"Really?"

She nodded, knocked back another mouthful of wine, then came over to my side of the table and wrapped her arms around me, throwing us into another kiss. She tasted like white wine, the wine I couldn't have, but I could drink

Ginger all in while she trembled beneath my arms, strong and frail at the same time.

Eventually she pulled away. "Sorry, I've got to go to the bathroom."

"No problem, I've got to do the cleaning up or someone might think I was useless in the kitchen."

She pressed a kiss to my cheek. "No, you're very useful."

After I finished cleaning up, I leaned back against the countertops, admiring my handiwork. Still no Ginger.

I wandered down the hallway. The bathroom door was open, the room empty. Not a lot of other rooms in her apartment so I headed for the bedroom.

Slumped on the edge of the bed, Ginger was staring down at the floor like a zombie, her face tearstained, eyes bleary.

I stood in the doorway. "Ginger?"

Nothing.

Sliding onto the bed beside her, I pulled her close and held her. She started sobbing, her body shaking but at least she was doing something. I let her cry.

"I'm sorry," she said after a while.

"You've got nothing to be sorry for."

"What's it like?"

"You mean having AIH?"

"I don't know what it's like to live when you know you're terminal."

"Neither do I. I just do my best."

She cupped my jaw in her tiny hands and pressed her lips against mine. "You're an amazing person, Cooper."

I slid my hands onto her delicate waist. "You're kind of awesome yourself, Ginger Lee."

Hooking her fingertips under the hem of my T-shirt, she pulled it over my head. "So many tattoos." She kissed my shoulder, made her way over my collarbone to my chest, then tossed her head back. "So irresponsible."

"I'll give you irresponsible." I pulled her across the middle of the bed, and took off her shirt. Peppering her neck with little kisses, my hands wandered over her waist, her boobs, her back, so I could undo the damn bra.

I stayed nuzzling into her neck. "I'm sorry I didn't tell you sooner. Sorry I didn't tell you before we fell in love with each other."

She pushed me away, an evil smile on her face, a glint in her eyes. "So big headed. Who says I'm in love with you?"

I slid the strap of her bra over one shoulder, then the other, watched the cup come loose. She tossed it aside, struggling to get the rest of her clothes off while I took her nipple into my mouth, first one, then the other. Those beautiful breasts. She thought they were small. She had it the wrong way around. It was the rest of her that was petite. Long, smooth legs, a tiny waist, flat stomach, pretty shoulders, pretty everything.

Man, I had way too many clothes on. I shucked off my pants, couldn't get them off fast enough, grabbing a condom in the process. She wrapped her little hand around me. I gasped, ready to explode. Not yet, not till I was inside her.

Ginger took it a step further, wrapped her mouth around me and I was a goner, absolutely nothing I could do. There was only her and me and my dick. My orgasm rocketed through me. She lay down beside me while I recovered.

Problem was, with Ginger beside me, I didn't want to recover. I wanted more. Always more.

"You should be naked all the time," I whispered.

I kissed her, my mouth on hers, on her nipples. I loved taking them into my mouth. I headed lower but she pulled me up, her hands digging into my shoulders.

"Now."

One word. An instruction. Her need as desperate as mine. When I entered her, it was like coming home. This was meant to be. We would always be together even if 'always' wasn't a long time.

Together. She climaxed first, a shrill cry escaping her lips, and I followed quickly.

If only life could always be this good. If only it was always me and her, like this, raw and unadulterated. This was what I wanted—to make the most of every moment, to make love to Ginger, to live life to the fullest.

I lay beside her on my side, stroking her hair, so smooth, so perfect like the rest of her. A tear escaped through her closed eye and ran down to her hairline. Then another.

I kissed her temple. "Don't cry, baby."

Her eyes sprung open as she edged up onto one elbow and held my gaze. "I'm not done with you yet, Cooper."

This won't be our last time. I didn't say it because one day there'd be a time that was our last. She took the lead. We rolled around together. I couldn't get enough of her. I'd never get enough.

A pang stabbed at my heart, beautiful and sad at the same time. We might not have long together.

But we'd have love. Plenty of love.

CHAPTER TEN

Ginger

I wished I could change the date of Grandmother's birthday lunch, wished I could change a lot of things, but so much was out of my hands.

Since I'd already had dinner with Cooper's folks, it didn't feel like I was imposing my family on him. Besides he'd already met my mom and Alistair, and the rest of the family was two thousand miles away on the other side of the country.

His hand in mine, I led him into Grandmother's dining room where Dad stood waiting in the doorway.

"Cooper, this is my dad, Benjamin."

This was followed by some serious handshaking.

Alistair pushed Maddy forward. The smile on her face told me she was dying to meet Cooper so I introduced them. She was the perfect daughter-in-law, well behaved and demure, and also an accountant. I was surrounded by them.

Sounds of excitement and maybe even some squawking emanated from the kitchen. Grandmother didn't quite make it to five feet in height but she made up for it in other ways.

"Halmoni, I'd like you to meet Cooper."

I'd already briefed him that it'd be disrespectful for him to call her by anything other than the Korean word for grandmother, and that using her Christian name would put him close to death.

Halmoni wrapped her arms around his waist, gripping him like a wrestler. Cooper returned the hug with one arm, the other holding her birthday present.

Eventually she let go. "So nice to meet you. You're special. That's why we invite you."

"Um, thank you." Cooper handed her a gift. "Happy birthday."

I placed my gift with the others on the sideboard for her to open later. Meanwhile Halmoni blushed, not something I'd seen often, as she unwrapped the package and held out a white baseball tee with red sleeves and 'The Merchants of Menace' written in Korean script, or at least I assumed that's what it was.

Smiling and still gasping, Halmoni zipped into the kitchen and came back seconds later modeling the T-shirt to a small round of applause. She did the wrestler-thing again, giving Cooper another hug.

More introductions followed as two elderly Korean neighbors walked in. I took solace in the presence of people, forced myself to act as if nothing was wrong, regardless of how much I was dying on the inside.

Mom had helped Halmoni with the extendable dining table and setting up the room but Halmoni always insisted on doing all the cooking herself. With one exception.

I motioned for Cooper to follow so I could put the

apple pie in the kitchen. Though not very Korean, this was Halmoni's weakness. I placed it in the refrigerator.

Cooper pointed. "If that's the fridge, then what's that?"

"The kim chi fridge."

He raised his eyebrows. "Your grandmother has a separate fridge for kim chi?"

"Boy, do you have a lot to learn. Halmoni has another fridge in the garage too."

"Really? But you said your grandfather passed away and that she lives alone."

I grabbed his arm. "We've gotta get out of here. Halmoni won't like you being in her kitchen."

"Sure."

After some more conversation, we settled around the table. I offered to help with preparations but Halmoni insisted she and Mom would do everything and that I should sit next to my young man. Dad sat on the other side of Cooper, Alistair and Maddy opposite us.

"So how come Halmoni gets the cool T-shirt?" Alistair put on his hurt face.

"When you're seventy-three, I might get one for you too," Cooper said.

My brother's eyes darted from side to side. "Seriously, I'd love one of those T-shirts. I can't tell you how much it'd mean."

"I'll see what I can do."

I shot my brother a sly smile. "Anything else you'd like? Any other little gifts?"

"Come on, Ginger," he said. "You get to see him every day. This is still a big thing for me."

"For me too," Dad butted in. "I've been reading a bit

about the music industry, 360 deals, and how they work. Sounds like daylight robbery to me."

Cooper turned to him. "We don't have a 360 deal."

I nudged him. "What's that?"

"It means the record company takes a hefty percentage of profits from merchandise, tours, endorsements, TV appearances, stuff like that."

"But they've got nothing to do with the merchandise," I said. "They just put your records out there."

He nodded. "Exactly." Then to my father. "We've got a brilliant manager who secured a sensational deal for us right from the start. Avoided all that sort of crap. I don't even know how he did it."

"Excellent," Dad said. "There's serious money in merchandising and endorsements. How about songwriting royalties? How does that work for you?"

"Dad," I said loudly. "You're asking a lot of nosy questions."

"What?" He looked offended. "I'm an accountant. The numbers and the business side of things are interesting to me."

"It's okay." Cooper turned to my dad. "But I'd love to hear more about you and what Ginger and Alistair were like growing up."

The inevitable embarrassing childhood stories followed, not that I minded too much. It filled me with warmth to see the smile on Cooper's face. Helped me to ignore the angst in my heart.

Once again, I offered to help and was refused while Mom and Halmoni brought various plates to the table. Cooper stared at the offerings, his eyes widening.

"With Korean food, it's all about the side dishes," I

said. "Halmoni's very proud of her kim chi. You'll have to try that. And a bit of everything else."

Dad poured Cooper a soju, a kind of vodka, holding the glass out. "This goes with the pork belly. It's my favorite."

Cooper shook his head. "Thanks, but I don't drink."

Dad straightened in shock. "You don't drink?"

They don't know. My gut twisted, anxiety simmering in my stomach. I tried to forget, tried to act normal, but couldn't.

Sucking in a deep breath, I changed the subject, explaining the different types of kim chi—radish, cabbage, and cucumber—and pointing out the various side dishes.

"That's my favorite. Lotus root. Loads of soy. Crunchy. Delicious."

Cooper watched the others. "Everyone's just digging in with their chopsticks."

"Yeah. That's how we do it. It's all about sharing."

He lowered his voice. "The double dipping is a bit weird. When it comes to sharing anything, I'm always so careful because of my immune system."

My heart clenched. I'd done this all wrong, brought him here, hadn't thought this through, and now he was putting himself at risk. What's more, there was no way my family would understand.

"I don't know what to do," I said.

He reached across for some barbecued chicken. "Screw my immune system."

I did the same and ate slowly, not tasting much at all.

"You know," he said. "I think the garlic and chili in this stuff would kill any germs anyway. I'm going to dig in."

Such a good sport, despite everything, and such a wonderful person. Tears sprang to my eyes but I held them back.

"Next weekend, let's make it just you and me," I said.

He grinned. "I won't object."

"We can go to the desert for the day, the two of us. I know a spot fairly close to the city, not too far if we need to come back, and we don't need to camp out or anything. There's something I want to show you. Not scenery, not exactly. It's kind of a ghost town."

"Sounds great."

Cooper helped himself to more chicken, seemed to enjoy that a lot more than the lotus root. Still, I had to hand it to him, he tried a bit of everything, with the exception of the alcohol. Such a trooper.

After we finished eating, Cooper glanced at Halmoni gathering up dishes at the other end of the table. He pushed his chair back and reached across for a couple of empty dishes.

"No, no," Alistair said. "You don't need to do that."

I shot him a dirty look. "Because the women do all the cleaning up as well as the cooking."

"That's not it." My brother threw his hands up. "Okay, find out for yourself then."

Cooper was already on his feet and heading for the kitchen with the dirty plates. Alistair and Dad kept talking so I asked Maddy how she was doing.

"Sure you don't feel outnumbered?" I asked.

She smiled. "Not at all. The food's fantastic and I'm happy to sit back and take it all in."

My old fears and insecurities flooded me, but I held them at bay. Even though she was the one who wasn't

Korean, I felt like the odd one out, the one who wasn't Korean enough, who hadn't followed the accepted path and who was now hiding something.

Cooper shuffled back, sitting down in a hurry.

"Everything okay?" I asked.

"Yeah, sure. Halmoni kicked me out of the kitchen, told me I had to sit down. I'm just being obedient."

Later, Halmoni brought the apple pie to the table and I served it with ice cream. A hit, if I did say so myself.

We'd been at it for several hours. Dad had already moved away to talk to the elderly neighbors in Korean, and Mom was deep in conversation with Alistair and Maddy.

Out of nowhere, my chest squeezed, my breaths coming short and fast. Cooper, my beautiful Cooper. I could almost forget what he'd told me. Almost. And then it'd come back to me again, the memory acute, the pain sharp.

I turned to look at him, Mitch's face flashing before me. My heart stopped, then started again. Why now? Why Mitch? When that was so long ago.

Cooper reached for my arm. "Are you okay?"

"Yes. No. I'm not sure."

"Let's go outside for a bit."

He helped me up, ushering me ahead so I could lead the way to the patio where we sat on the outdoor chairs, the summer heat soaking through us right away.

Cooper leaned closer. "What happened back there?"

"It was just a weird moment of déjà vu or something."

"Yeah?" He waited.

"When I was at school, I had a boyfriend who—" I couldn't keep the hitch from my voice "—he died."

Cooper slid his hand onto my lap. "Oh, Ginger. I had no idea."

"He wasn't my first boyfriend, but he was my first."

"Okay."

"First time I had sex, first guy who really meant something. First love. I guess that was the big thing."

First heartbreak, the part I didn't say. Cooper nodded for me to continue.

"Mitch died from a brain aneurism. It was no one's fault, nothing anyone could have done, even though his mom was a doctor. And it was quick, so quick. One evening, he said he had a headache, went to the bathroom, and collapsed. Just like that."

There was more to it, though, always more. Maybe if things had panned out differently, I would've been more truthful, but his mom had insisted I go along with her suggestion and I'd been in no position to argue. After that, things had simply stayed that way. She'd liked me and had always wanted the best even if that wasn't the way things turned out.

"Ginger, I'm sorry." Cooper's voice cracked. "About everything."

Were we still talking about Mitch? I didn't know.

"It still hurts," I said. "He was only seventeen. Way too young."

Like you, Cooper, like you're too young. My heart twisted, my chest squeezing, a splutter escaping my lips.

He took my hand into his. "I know what you're thinking."

I shook my head, couldn't bring myself to speak.

"And I can't..." His voice trailed off, his eyes sweeping across Halmoni's small, well-tended vegetable patch. Avoiding me. Avoiding my gaze.

"You can't what?"

A muscle in his jaw flinched. "I wish things didn't have to be this way."

So do I, Cooper. My throat tight, I could barely swallow. I wished we could go back in time, but even that wouldn't be enough. We needed an alternate universe, a place where we were together, just me and Cooper. And no disease.

"I don't know what the right thing to do is anymore," he said. "I put on a brave face and sometimes I'm doing a brilliant job and other times I don't know what the fuck I'm doing."

"You're living, Cooper. You're doing your best."

"Your family thinks I'm some sort of celebrity."

I shrugged. "Well, you are."

"I'm not a rock star, even if I used to act like a spoiled shit. I'm just a guy who plays in a band. Or I used to be. I'm not that anymore."

I slid my hand across to his knee. "You're still The Merchants' drummer."

"For now. Not for long. It's the only thing I've ever known." He gritted his teeth. "There are a couple of things to look forward to—we're playing at Morgan Masterson's birthday party and also at the re-opening of The Swamp."

I searched for something positive. "There are other things you can do too. You had that idea about scholarships, didn't you?"

"Yeah, and I've got a meeting lined up with someone from Frankston University to discuss some stuff. That's fine. The problem is, I don't have much time to still be a drummer. My time for that has nearly run out. I'm trying to be practical. I don't want to hold the other guys back but I'm finding it really hard to be so fucking gracious all the time."

I squeezed his knee. "But you *are* incredibly gracious. That's just you, Cooper. And if you lose it sometimes, that's absolutely fine too."

He looked down at my hand. "This is only the beginning, Ginger. It's going to get a shitload worse. It won't be like with your brother. I'm not getting better."

Pain ripped through my chest. One day I'd lose him, one day soon. I'd never get used to this, didn't even know how I'd get through it, only that I had to. Tears burned at the back of my eyes. *I can't do this.* Not here, not now, maybe not ever.

I kneeled on the paving in front of Cooper, slid my hands up onto his shoulders as I forced a smile to my face. "It's not all bad. My family loves you."

He looked into my eyes. "And what about you, Ginger?"

I shrugged, played it cool. "I'll put up with you."

I pulled his head down over mine, my mouth on his, kissing him hard. He tasted like apples and ice cream, his lips supple, his hands on my waist making me feel small.

There'd be a time I wouldn't have his kisses anymore. I started choking, tears threatening to fall so I swallowed back the sorrow and forced myself to my feet. I had to get out of here.

"Come on." I pulled Cooper up behind me. "We can't stay out here all day."

I couldn't believe this had all happened so fast, couldn't let him know my pain when he had such huge problems of his own.

And I couldn't let him know how much I loved him.

It'd only be putting myself at even more risk.

CHAPTER ELEVEN

Cooper

I looked around the abandoned town. "How have I never heard of this place before when I've lived in Frankston all my life?"

Dilapidated buildings, little gray boxes with flat roofs, sat on flat sandy soil. Weeds grew through cracked concrete roads that had barely been driven on in decades. Utility poles protruded from the ground, though the power lines had long ago disintegrated or been removed.

Ginger wiped a rivulet of sweat from her forehead. "I guess most people have forgotten about it."

"So how did you even know it was here?"

"I've spend a lot of time in the desert looking for locations, photographing the rocks and plants and scenery. Then one day I decided to get off the main road and see what was here."

"It feels like a movie set."

"Like time stopped."

If there was a post apocalyptic world, this is what it'd look like—the sun pounding down on the desert, the remnants of a past civilization turning to dust.

People had lived here once. It'd been a town, a community. Would it still be here in fifty years? In a hundred years, would another couple like us chance upon the foundations of buildings that were long gone and wonder what had happened?

Ginger crouched down, her loose white shirt billowing with the movement. I presumed she'd worn it to keep the sun off her arms and shoulders. Thankfully she wasn't concerned about the sun on her legs, so I could admire them in the denim cutoffs.

She pointed her camera at the bare pavement, only it wasn't bare. A gray-brown lizard had its head up, surveying its surroundings. That thing had to be at least a foot long. I stayed quiet so as not to disturb it. Or Ginger.

After she took the shot, the animal scampered off in the other direction.

Ginger stood up. "A long-nosed leopard lizard."

"How do you even know that?"

"You'll pick up on this stuff if you keep hanging around me." She whacked me on the arm as we kept wandering. "I know what you mean, though. My mom isn't exactly an expert on the names of native fauna, so it's not something I grew up with. Luckily I can look these things up on Google."

One of the buildings had its windows boarded up but the doors had been ripped off so you could see through it. Ginger took shots from a few different angles, then asked me to lean in the doorway at the far end. After she'd taken some more photos, I came back to look at the screen on the back of the camera.

"I don't know how you do it." I stared at the abandoned shack, then motioned to the camera. "You make it into art."

She smiled. "Thanks. I wanted your silhouette in there to add a human element, to reflect that people used to live here once."

Which was exactly what I'd been thinking. Talk about being on the same wavelength.

Unlike Ginger, I hadn't covered up, wearing a sweat stained T-shirt and shorts. Any longer out here and the bare skin of my arms and the back of my neck would be red raw.

"You know how you wanted to set out early before it got too hot?" I asked.

"Yeah."

"It didn't work."

"Come on." She motioned for me to follow. "We could've been here a couple of hours earlier if I'd had my way."

I'd tried to tell her I played in a band, that people like me didn't do early mornings and that dawn was absolutely out of the question unless we approached it from the other side, staying up all night. A crappy argument because she was right and we should've got up even earlier.

Her car was parked in the middle of the street because, hey, you could park wherever you wanted here. She opened the trunk, passed the cooler for me to carry, and pulled out a picnic blanket.

"We might as well eat in the shade." She led the way to the shack she'd just photographed, probably because the roof was still in tact providing shade, then spread the picnic blanket across the dusty, deteriorated concrete. "We can get the through-draft between the two open doors."

I deposited the cooler, sat down, and wiped the sweat

from my face. "Yep, so cool."

Sitting cross-legged opposite me, she shoved a bottle of water into my hand. "You'd better behave or you won't get any lunch."

I knocked back half a bottle, a chunk of ice clunking around in the bottle as I drank, the cold water refreshing as it slid down my throat. Ginger had thought of everything.

As I was peering into the cooler, she passed across a sandwich.

"Italian style," she said. "Mixed meats, and I'm relieved it's still cold."

I took a bite. "Ah, the Panini Queen. I thought you were Korean."

She produced a small container and chopsticks. "With a side of kim chi."

"For me too?"

"Of course." She picked up some of the fermented cabbage with her chopsticks. "I thought sharing would be okay since we've already shared quite a lot."

We ate in silence, the companionable kind. The hot kind if I was going to be honest because the breeze Ginger had mentioned was purely in her imagination.

After a while she said, "I really wanted to show you this. It's not picturesque, not exactly, but it's so stark and strange with a beauty of its own. Doesn't matter that we can't trek to the deepest, darkest desert and stay overnight." She threw her hands up. "I mean, how many people get to see this? And you get it. You really get it."

"I do, Ginger. I feel it." I looked down at the empty wrappings from our sandwiches, then back up at her. "What else is going on with deepest, darkest Ginger?"

She sat very still, her hands resting on her knees, but something changed in her eyes and in the set of her pretty mouth.

"You've been through a lot," I said. "With your brother, with Mitch, and now with me. You already lost one boyfriend."

She squeezed her eyes shut, opened them. "Don't say it."

A pang of guilt shot through me. I'd crossed a line, causing her even more pain.

"Mitch wasn't my boyfriend," she said.

I frowned, certain she'd said that he was.

She cleared her throat. "When he died, he wasn't my boyfriend. He died suddenly, that part's true. We'd been together for six months and I wanted to make him love me but I couldn't. Things had been rocky between us for a couple of weeks, maybe longer. Deep inside I knew, but didn't want to face it."

"It happens like that when you love someone."

"The night before he died, he broke off with me. I was so upset, devastated, heartbroken. That night, no one knew he was going to have an aneurism or that he only had hours to live." Her voice faltered. "It was a Saturday so he hadn't seen anyone from school yet. No one knew we'd broken up except his parents. He'd told them already."

"I'm sorry, Ginger."

"His mom always adored me and didn't want to think Mitch had dumped me. She said no one else needed to know, that for all intents and purposes I was still his girlfriend, that I should always remember him that way. It didn't seem right to argue with her, and I was in shock."

Ginger's lower lip trembled. "I know Mitch didn't mean for it to happen that way, but he broke my heart twice—first when he split up with me and then again when he died."

I shifted closer, held her in my arms while she gripped my sweaty T-shirt for dear life.

"I'm not going to cry," she mumbled. "I've cried enough."

"Hey, my shirt's wet already. A few tears wouldn't make any difference."

She nudged me away. "You can always make me smile."

That wasn't true. Not always.

"I had a friend who died too," I said. "I'm not comparing it with your loss. I was in my twenties, better able to cope, and this wasn't the love of my life. You've probably heard of him, Dave Tournier."

"From Red Flag? The guitar player?"

"Yeah. He had hepatitis."

Different sort from mine. He had a completely different response from mine too. He hadn't cleaned up his act. Kept on using. Got sicker.

A furrow formed in Ginger's brow. "I thought it was a heroine overdose. That's what the papers said."

"Dave's symptoms were getting bad. The poor guy had been vomiting blood, the beginning of the end. He was bloated, muscles cramping up, and yellow from the jaundice. Discharged himself from the hospital and then he chose a different way out. He always said he wanted to go out on a high."

My gut clenched. I'd seen him, seen how bad the disease was getting, so I knew what I was in for. I couldn't kid myself I'd die peacefully in my sleep surrounded by people who loved me.

"I was there the first night he ever shot up," I said. "Backstage after a gig. I was popping pills that night, buying rounds of drinks, some girl hanging off my arm. I tried to tell him smack was a dumb shit idea. Didn't try hard enough because I wanted to get wasted as quickly as possible."

"That doesn't make it your fault."

"Not exactly." I held her gaze. "Not that far off either."

"I'm sorry about your friend." She slid her hand onto my shoulder. "But he's not you. He's a different person. You don't have to be like him."

"I know that."

"You're scared."

"Oh, yeah. Like you wouldn't believe."

I swallowed back the fear. Sure, I was scared of death and even more frightened of what it'd be like near the end when I'd be a shell of a man, unable to wash or feed myself, maybe unable to speak, and God only knows what else. But that wasn't the main thing.

Most of all, I was scared for my family and for the people who loved me. Because they'd be in agony, my suffering nothing compared to theirs. They were the ones who'd go through the worst, who'd never forget, who had to keep on living. My parents especially, they'd never get over it.

And now I could add Ginger to that list.

Despair sank deep into my bones. What had I done? How could I put her through this when she'd already lost one boyfriend? Yet how could I possibly let her go?

Something twisted inside me, pain shooting through my chest. It didn't matter how strong I tried to be, it could only last for so long.

Ginger nuzzled closer. "You're not alone, though. You'll never be alone."

"There's so much that's wrong. I'm so careful all the time, eating properly, living a clean lifestyle, trying to take care of myself."

"That's a good thing. Don't put yourself down."

"I can't even camp out in the desert with you like you wanted. I mean, we can take other vacations, just not that one."

She pulled away, a smile on her face. "Then you'll have to make it five-star. Nothing less will do."

I pressed a kiss to her lips. "You deserve five stars."

She deserved a hell of a lot better than she was getting. When I thought about what this was doing to Ginger, it felt as if my heart was being ripped from my rib cage. Sometimes it was so hard to do the right thing or even know what that was.

Her eyes widened. "One more thing I have to show you."

I motioned around me, trying to make light of it. "But what could be better than these luxurious surroundings?"

She stood, started packing up the lunch things. "Come on."

I folded up the blanket "Where are we going?"

"To the drive-in."

But we'd already seen the back of that thing when we'd driven in. It was big and kind of hard to miss. Sometimes I didn't know what was going through that pretty head of hers, only that I'd go along with nearly anything she said.

I picked up the cooler. "Are we driving there?"

"Yeah, of course we have to *drive* to the drive-in." She laughed. "What on earth were you thinking?"

We piled our gear into the trunk of the car. Ginger got into the driver's seat, insisting I close my eyes—so I could get the full impact, she said. The drive took all of about two minutes until she pulled up, leaving the engine running.

I opened my eyes. And laughed. A couple of palm trees flanked the big screen, stark against the backdrop of a blue sky, the word CLOSED printed across the screen in big red letters. As if no one could work that out.

Ginger grinned. "Isn't it cool?"

The smile on her face gave me so much joy. She was like a little kid sometimes.

"It's cool, all right."

"It's amazing to think people had driven here, like we did, only they were coming for a big night out. They would've bought popcorn from the kiosk and sat in their cars with the speakers on, watching movies on the big screen. Little kids would probably have fallen asleep in the back seat. Teenagers would probably have made out. People would've watched the latest movies."

I leaned across, pressing little kisses to her neck. "Have you ever made out at the drive-in?"

An innocent expression on her face. "I've never even *been* to a drive-in."

"Well, there's a first time for everything."

Her lips curled to a sultry smile, her hand edging toward the ignition.

I placed my hand on her arm. "Hey, don't turn off the engine. We need the air conditioning."

She raised one perfectly arched eyebrow. "You think you're that hot?"

"I know I am."

Not me, Ginger. You're the one who's hot and beautiful, cute and sexy, everything a man could want.

I covered her mouth with mine, kissed her deep and hard, our tongues rolling around each other. Reaching down, I reclined my seat back as far as it would go.

"Whoa, smooth move," she said.

"You ain't seen nothin' yet."

I ripped off my T-shirt, tossing it aside. She pulled apart the sides of her white shirt so I slid it off her shoulders and threw it onto the back seat. Got rid of the bra too. The two of us fumbling, we shucked our pants off, and I dug a condom out of the pocket.

Ginger slung one leg across to sit on my lap, her skin glowing with perspiration, her eyes glinting with lust. Sweaty bodies sliding against each other. Sexual desire building. Cramped, no room in here, no comfort, only the burning in my groin. And hers.

Sex, yes. And more, much more.

After we were done, Ginger stayed on my lap, her boobs glistening with sweat. Lips parted, still breathing hard, she pressed some damp strands of hair behind her ear. Her ponytail was still in tact, mostly.

"I've got the air conditioning blasting into my back." She tossed her head back. "I don't know if that's good or bad."

"Told you I was hot."

She laughed, bumping into the steering wheel as she made her way over to the driver's seat, then laughed again. My heart melted. She could always do that to me.

Her eyes darted around the interior of the vehicle. "What've you done with my panties?"

"What have *I* done?"

She found her shirt instead, slipped that on. "Yes, that's what I said."

We fumbled around for our clothes, taking a hell of lot longer to pull them over our sweaty bodies than it had taken to get them off.

Leaning closer, I slid my hand onto the bare skin of her thigh. "I love you, Ginger."

Her lips parted, eyes wide as she stared at me in awe, her lower lip trembling.

"I don't know if it was love at first sight," I said. "But it wasn't far off. Within the first five minutes, maybe."

Tears tumbled down her cheeks. I wiped them off, pulled her close, pressed little kisses to her damp cheeks.

"I don't want to make you cry all the time. That's not what I'm here for."

"No, you're here for the mind-blowing sex." She hiccupped, her lips curving to a smile. "Anyway, these are happy tears. I've never felt this way before." Letting out a sob, she covered her mouth, looked down again.

I pressed my finger to her lips, then pulled her close and held her. "I've never felt this way before either."

She hadn't said she loved me too. Such a relief.

Because I could keep fooling myself that maybe she didn't.

CHAPTER TWELVE

Ginger

Cooper's sister asked me to bring along my camera but hadn't said why or what I was supposed to be photographing. Sitting around the dinner table at his parents' house after a delicious roast, I still didn't know why.

"Is Jack going to be much longer?" Cooper asked. "We need to get going soon."

Amy checked her phone. "He's on his way."

Stuck at the office, apparently, not that I necessarily thought that was a good enough excuse when his family was waiting. Or Amy's family, as the case may be.

Cooper raised his eyebrows. "Why the mystery, sis?"

She leaned back. "Why the rush?"

Perhaps because The Merchants were playing a few songs at a private birthday party for Morgan Masterson tonight. I knew him vaguely, having met him years ago at his recording studio.

And now here I was at Cooper's childhood home. I'd seen the photos in the living room so I could see the resemblance between Cooper and his sister. They had the same blue eyes, only hers were sparkling whereas Cooper's seemed dull.

He leaned back in his chair with a thump. "Come on, I've been hanging out for this gig. You know how I love this stuff."

His mother placed a hand on his arm. "Five more minutes won't kill you. Jack's nearly here."

Amy's phone vibrated on the table. Staring at it, she grinned as she got up. "That's him. Be right back."

After some whispering and shuffling in the hallway, she came back with Jack on her arm. To be fair, her husband looked frazzled as if he'd spent too long at the office, his white shirt creased, tie loosened. I got up as she introduced us.

"Nice to meet you." He stretched out his arm for a handshake.

"We have something to tell you." Amy couldn't stop beaming. Cooper didn't stop looking pissed off. She added, "I'm pregnant. We're having a baby."

Cooper's face was like a wipe in a movie, eyes lighting up, cheeks lifted, a huge smile, teeth gleaming. He got up, wrapped his arms around his sister, and swung her around.

"That's wonderful, sis." He held her at arm's length, then stepped across to hug Jack too, only his brother-in-law wasn't so good at reciprocating.

I'd brought the Lumix because I'd be taking photos at the party—and also for Amy—so I pulled it from my purse and got ready. My brain seemed to be working despite the fact I was bursting with joy for Amy. And I'd only just met her.

"I'm so happy for you." Cooper's mom let out a sob, tears tumbling down her cheeks. His dad put his arm around her and helped her up.

Amy was still beaming, an embarrassed smile on Jack's face. Cooper's dad went for some vigorous hand shaking with Jack. Meanwhile his mom clung to her daughter.

I took a couple of photos because I presumed this was what Amy wanted. It made me feel useful during this intimate, family moment.

While Amy and her mom were still in hug-mode, Cooper's dad said something to him, his eyes glimmering with emotion. Cooper pulled him into his embrace, the two of them gripping each other with their eyes closed. Just holding each other, not speaking.

I captured the moment, father and son together. It was like that with people you loved. You didn't always have to speak. Sometimes you just needed to be there.

After a while, Cooper's mom extracted herself from Amy's grip. "You know what, I need to sit down."

I pulled out a chair for her. "Let's get a group shot." I pointed to Cooper's dad. "Take a seat next to your wife, *grandpa.*"

"It's true." He sat down, put his arm around her. "We're going to be grandparents."

Amy stood in the middle at the back, her brother and husband beside her.

Cooper motioned toward me. "You have to be in the photo too."

The rest of the family insisted, so I set the camera onto the table on self-timer and joined them. Was I one of the family? Regardless of the answer, it was heartwarming to be included in this special moment.

Cooper nudged his brother-in-law. "So you finally got her knocked up, eh!"

We all laughed. The flash went off. I left the group to check the picture on the back of the camera. Perfect.

While I packed up my gear, they asked the usual questions. How far along was she? Eight weeks. A boy or a girl? Too soon to know and they didn't want to find out ahead of time anyway. Eventually Cooper said we had to get going.

Morgan's place was on the other side of town so we had quite a drive ahead of us, not that it mattered. We'd be late but not too late. Part of the reason Cooper wanted to get going was that he became fatigued early and couldn't handle late nights anymore. At least I knew what was going on with him now.

I took off as the traffic lights turned green. "You're going to be Uncle Cooper."

"Sure am. I don't think anyone has ever called my dad 'grandpa' before."

"He looked like he was in shock. You all did."

"In the best way possible."

Not like the shocking news Cooper had laid on them two years ago. The same news he'd given me recently. A pang gripped my heart at the thought of what he was going through, what was to come, the thought of losing him.

I indicated, changed lanes, forced myself to concentrate on driving.

"I'm so happy for Amy and Jack." After a while, Cooper added, "You like kids."

A statement or question, I wasn't sure which. "Yeah, I do."

"Do you think you'll have children one day?"

"The truth?" I swallowed the lump in my throat. "I can't imagine going through life without them."

"Me neither." With those two words, his voice cracked. Looking straight ahead at the road, I held back the tears welling in my eyes.

I bit my lip, searching for something to say that might make him feel better, but what could I say?

After a while, he said, "The irony is that if I hadn't got AIH, no way would I be considering anything to do with kids. No way in the world. I'd be thinking about recording and touring and the Flats Festival. I'd be hanging out with the guys. Yet the disease is the very reason…" His voice trailed off. "Ah, fuck it. Life's a bitch."

"I'm sorry, Cooper."

We drove the rest of the way in silence. I tried to concentrate on the road, tried to think about anything else except Cooper's condition. He didn't need to spell it out, didn't need to tell me he wouldn't be around to see his kids grow up if he had them. Might not even be around to see them go to school. For all I knew, he might not even be able to have children.

My heart clenched tighter. And me? What would I do?

I couldn't think about this now, not when we were supposed to be having a good time at a party. Some things were too hard to think about.

Cooper put his arm around me after we got out of the car. "Sorry to drag you down."

The street was packed with cars. Drum and bass filled the air, the sound of people chatting floating over the top.

"No, not at all," I lied.

"I want you to be happy."

"I am happy. It's just…"

"Yeah, I know." Cooper stopped at the bottom of the front path. "Do you know what I do when I go in to a party like this? I put on a mask." He shook the hair off his face, put on a grin.

"You look like a scary clown. I thought you were supposed to be a cool rock star." I frowned, a smile creeping to my lips. "Hey, I want a refund."

He took my hand and we walked up the front path together, a bouncer opening the front door for us. After that, we followed the noise to the rear of the house. And what a house.

People had gathered around a large island bench in the all-white kitchen, others on the leather sofas in the living area, the rest of the crowd spilling onto the patio where reflections from the pool rippled on the patio ceiling. A good sized crowd. Not too many people. But noisy, thanks to the sound bouncing off the hard surfaces.

"Cooper, my man, glad you could make it." Morgan Masterson squeezed Cooper's shoulder before turning to place a quick kiss on my cheek. "Lovely to see you too, Ginger."

His hair was a little too long, a few loose strands hanging over his forehead, reminiscent of an old movie star. Then it hit me.

"You're a dead ringer for Mickey Rourke," I said. "When he was young, that is, before the plastic surgery."

Morgan swept his hand toward me. "Has anyone told you that you look like Audrey Hepburn?"

"It's not me. It's the dress. Oh, and happy birthday."

Clearly the little black dress I was wearing had done the trick. A different LBD from the one I'd worn to Nick and Lily's wedding, a diamante necklace this time, same effect.

"Thank you." Morgan turned to Cooper. "We closed

off the theater room until you guys were ready to start playing."

"So I can see," he said.

Morgan excused himself, stepping away to greet another couple who'd walked in.

Cooper pressed a kiss to my cheek. "By the way, the dress is lovely, but it's *always* you, Ginger."

I squeezed his waist. "You're such a smoothie."

"I'm hoping I might get in if I play my cards right."

I laughed, pushed him away. "Not quite so smooth anymore!"

Nick and Lachie appeared, greeting me with a kiss on the cheek and Cooper with a whack on the back.

Lachie pushed back his long blond hair. "We're going to have to steal Cooper away from you soon."

Joel came up to us. "We should make a move, get started."

Lachie nodded. "Exactly what we were saying."

The other guys nodded in agreement.

Cooper pulled me close. "Are you going to be okay?"

"I've got my camera ready. You just go off and do your thing. You won't even notice I'm here."

As the boys left, Jess came bounding over and gave me a hug. It'd been a long time. I hadn't seen her since Nick and Lily's wedding.

"You should join us." She pointed across the room where Lily and Scarlett were waving wildly at me. I waved right back. Of course, the girlfriends hung out together. It made sense. And I was part of it.

"I'd love to." I longed to catch up with them, in fact. "But I want to take some band shots while they're setting up and maybe while they're playing."

She raised her eyebrows. "You still working on the photo book?"

"Yep."

I wandered across the room to the theater where the band had set up. The guys had pulled open the double doors, revealing a carpeted room with acoustic panels on the walls and ceiling, their gear already set up.

In the background, someone turned the music off or down, I couldn't tell which.

Nick slung his guitar strap over his head, said something that made Cooper laugh. I took a photo, capturing the casualness of the moment.

I was in my element here, a good place to be, a much better place than I'd been with Cooper in the car on the way over here. *Don't think about that.*

Besides, Cooper wasn't Mitch. The end had been so quick for him, no chance for goodbyes, no way to tell each other how we'd truly felt. Because he'd cared for me in his own way, I had to believe that. I swallowed the lump in my throat.

Settling behind the drum kit, Cooper shot me one of his killer smiles. My heart swelled for all the right reasons. With Cooper around, life just got a little bit better.

Behind me, the crowd was still chattering while in front of me, Cooper banged the snare. Hard. Did a quick drum roll. The chatter turned to a murmur as people moved closer, watching from the living area. I stayed to one side where I'd be able to take photos.

Lachie let it rip with the first riffs of a familiar song that took me a moment to recognize. Then it came to me. An old Beatles song, *Birthday*, now that'd make Nick happy since he was their biggest fan. Judging by the look on

Morgan's face, it was making him pretty happy too.

They launched into some Merchants' songs. I glanced around at the crowd, the looks on their faces telling me this was exactly what they wanted. The band played a few more songs and I took some more photos, then wandered to the other side of the room to stand with Jess and the girls.

I absolutely couldn't stop my toes from tapping, my body swaying with the next song, *Always at Midnight*, an old favorite. That was the thing. As much as I loved my camera, I didn't want to live life only through its lens. I had to make sure I enjoyed every moment.

Still, I did want to take a few more photos so after the song finished, I found a spot to one side, crouching down to get a good angle and got a shot at the exact moment that sweat sprayed from Nick's face. So rock 'n' roll.

For some reason, it sounded like the song was losing momentum. Cooper missed a beat, or at least that was what I thought happened. They kept going but the song sounded a bit weird. Like The Merchants had been set to slow motion.

Something dark dribbled down Cooper's chin. I straightened my back. Nick glanced around to see what was going on, did a double take.

Cooper's body convulsed. Blood, he vomited blood. Fear rocketed through me. He smashed the drums, slower still, like an Energizer Bunny on its last legs. Nick yelled something to the boys.

Blood poured down Cooper's shirt. I stood up, leaning against the wall behind me. My legs wouldn't hold.

"That's it for tonight, folks," Nick said into the microphone. "Our drummer's doing his best Alice Cooper impersonation. All part of the show. See you later."

Lachie and Joel got rid of their gear and sprang across to Cooper, one of them on either side, while I stood gasping for air.

Nick led the way, the other two guys holding Cooper up as he walked, while I trailed behind, my heart racing, none of this quite registering. Morgan pulled open a door, motioning us into the bedroom.

The guys helped Cooper sit on the bed, but he shook them off, his eyes glazed, shoulders slumped. He wiped the blood from his chin, some of it anyway, probably didn't see the blood down the front of his shirt.

I dropped onto the bed, sliding my arm around him. I pressed little kisses to his cheek, his temple. He seemed too weak to respond. My heart fell a little further.

I still had the camera around my neck, my purse slung over my shoulder. My hands shaking, I pulled out my phone and called 911 but it felt like a nightmare where my phone was too slow and my fingers wouldn't move.

"I need paramedics," I spluttered into the phone.

My heart gripped with fear, I couldn't think, couldn't breathe, could barely speak to the 911 dispatcher. A calm voice at the other end asked a couple of questions.

"My boyfriend is vomiting blood. This is an emergency. He's sick. Auto-immune hepatitis. He needs help. *Now*."

"Cirrhosis," Cooper croaked. "Tell them it's cirrhosis."

I told them. The dispatcher asked for a couple more details.

"The address?" I looked around, my eyes pleading. "What's the address?"

Morgan took the phone from me, gave them the

answers. Thank goodness, he had his head screwed on.

I was still clutching Cooper with one arm. Shit, what if this had happened when we were in the desert an hour and a half's drive from Frankston? What would I have done then? What would *we* have done?

He convulsed, vomited again, had no chance of even making it to the bathroom. My stomach twisted into an enormous knot, despair sinking deep into my bones.

Morgan appeared, handed me a towel so I tried to clean Cooper up a little. Breathing hard, he snatched the towel, sick as a dog but determined.

I felt a reassuring hand on my shoulder and looked up at Jess.

"I'll stand outside and wave down the paramedics when they arrive," she said. "Lily and Scarlett are in the hall if you need them."

No room for them in here, not with the guys from the band and Morgan taking up all the space. Cooper's friends, people who loved him, who were taking care of him. And me. I loved him too. The pain ripping through my chest left me in no doubt.

He vomited again. More blood. My heart thumped wildly, crashing against the walls of my chest. How could he be losing more blood? Where were the paramedics?

Nick and Lachie were trying to talk to Cooper.

"I'm okay." He shook them off. "Where's Ginger?"

I dropped to my knees in front of him. "I'm here, Cooper."

He seemed so calm. No, not calm. Weak. And pale. So much blood lost.

Panic shot through me all over again. I hadn't truly believed this could happen.

My beautiful Cooper. Disappearing before my eyes.

CHAPTER THIRTEEN

Cooper

Day three in the hospital. The food was fine, the nurses were lovely, the doctors even better, and I couldn't wait to get the hell out of here.

Dread had weighed me down from the minute I'd woken up, though less than yesterday morning and the day before. I'd been through this before when I first received the diagnosis of AIH and knew how it worked. I'd eventually end up feeling less shit. That was the best you could hope for when you knew you were going to die.

Ginger sat by the bed on a padded vinyl chair, the sort you only found in hospitals and offices because no one would buy something like that for their house.

My throat hurt like hell thanks to yesterday's endoscopy, a procedure where they stuck a tube down my gullet to take a good look around. But I couldn't let the pain show in front of Ginger.

"You missed the specialist." I adjusted the pillows behind my back. "He came early."

She straightened. "Early?"

I shrugged. "I know, doctors are always running late,

every day except today."

Her eyes widened. "But I canceled a shoot so I could hear what he had to say."

"What? You shouldn't have canceled a job because of me, Ginger. You've still got to work. Life goes on, remember."

I couldn't bear the thought of her putting her life on hold for me, not when she'd need to work and keep her business going. She had a future, and I couldn't let her screw that up.

"You don't look happy, Ginger."

Tears welled in her eyes. "I'm trying, Cooper, truly I am but it's hard to keep smiling when you're so ill."

And I'd done this to her. Dragged her down to my level when this was the last thing I wanted. I didn't want it for myself either, but there were some things I had no choice about.

What's more, this wasn't the end of the bad shit to do with my AIH. It was only the beginning.

I pressed my eyes shut, my gut twisting. I'd seen what had happened to Dave before he'd ended it all, so I had a pretty good idea what was coming. And it was *not* pretty.

"Cooper?"

"I'm fine. Did I mention I'll be out in a couple of days?"

Her eyes lit up. "So soon? That's great."

I slung my legs over the other side of the bed so I could make my way to the window. I'd ditched the hospital gown for a T-shirt and sweatpants that at least made me feel half human. Yesterday I'd even made Ginger laugh when I'd told her the gown didn't go with my tats. It was something.

"It's weird," she said. "How you had no symptoms before this. Or hardly any."

"That's the way this disease works."

For now. There'd be a truckload of symptoms coming soon.

I stared out of the window, seeing but not seeing.

When I'd spewed blood at Morgan's party, that was down to cirrhosis of the liver. I'd been prepared—or as prepared as anyone could be—because the doctors had primed me that that part would be coming sooner or later. I'd hoped later.

It made no difference that I hadn't touched a drop of alcohol since my diagnosis, that I was taking all my medication religiously and doing all the right things. It sure as hell didn't matter that I was only twenty-five.

I'd been through a lot of this with Ginger already, but she'd seemed so hopeful that I hadn't had the heart to give her all the bad news at once. She understood the basics about cirrhosis and how it was caused by too much scar tissue on the liver, which meant the organ couldn't perform its functions.

Then there was the part I hadn't told her yet—that the five to ten year prognosis went out the door if you'd already progressed to the stage of cirrhosis. Nope, I wouldn't have anywhere near that long.

It sucked the air right out of me. Stomach churning, gut wrenching, I swallowed back the fear. I had to while Ginger was here.

I cleared my throat, kept staring out the window. "At Morgan's party when I was vomiting blood, a big bleed would have meant death."

"But it *wasn't* a big bleed." Indignation filled her voice.

"There's no fixing this, no cure, no way out. The disease has progressed too far now."

I should go to her, take her in my arms. I should be a better man. Instead, it was as much as I could do to hold back the tears burning at the back of my eyes. I forced myself to be strong, to get my shit together. God knows Ginger deserved better.

"The doctors talked about a liver transplant," she said in a small voice.

I turned. She looked so small scrunched in the chair, her ponytail messy, swamped in the loose shirt she wore. I wasn't used to seeing her all mussed up.

Taking her hands into mine, I sat on the high hospital bed opposite her, gave her the attention she needed.

"It's not that straightforward. There's a system. You jockey for position to get higher up the list, and they're very strict with their criteria."

She held my gaze. "But money's not a problem for you. That's got to help. You've had such good medical care until now, you told me that."

"With a transplant, it makes no difference how much money you have. The liver goes to the person who needs it the most. It wouldn't be fair if they gave it to me because I'm rich." My voice starting to crack, I waited a moment. "People who are going to die first are at the top of the list. That's how dire your situation needs to be to get a liver transplant."

Tears tumbled down her pretty cheeks. I didn't go through the rest, the complications of a liver transplant, the risk of rejection, the shortened lifespan.

"But that's the closest they have to a cure," she said. "And you're on the list. There's nothing to say you won't be one of those people who gets a liver transplant. Whatever happens, we'll work something out."

My throat tightened. Why was there even a 'we'? Why wasn't she young and carefree anymore like she'd been before we met? I'd ruined her, given her love and one day my gift to her would be death.

Way to go, Cooper. How fucking selfish.

I hadn't known things would turn out this way with her. I'd never been in love, not like this anyway, despite the fact I'd had plenty of girlfriends and had even been married. I was used to girls who came and went.

Only now I didn't want to let her go, couldn't bear the thought.

I hated looking down at her from the hospital bed so I dropped to my knees in front of her, my hands sliding onto her lap. So warm, so soft, she was everything I'd ever wanted and more than I'd ever known I could have.

"Ginger, you're so young."

"Not that much younger than you."

"You've got everything going for you. You should find someone whole and healthy and make a life for yourself."

"No." Her voice wobbled.

"Your parents didn't raise you so you could screw your life up like this."

I'd already told her there was no point trying to hide this anymore, not from family, not from the people who mattered.

She shook my hands off her lap. "Do you know what my mom said? That I hadn't changed since I was ten years old when I was looking after Alistair and she'd tell me to go out and play, only I wouldn't leave my brother. She knows I'll always stay. She didn't even try to talk me out of it." Ginger's voice cracked. "She told me to follow my heart."

"I don't believe it was that simple." My throat aching, I forced my voice to stay even. "Was your mom crying as she said this? Were tears streaming down her face?"

Ginger didn't say anything. I could guess her mother's pain in watching what her poor daughter was going through.

I gritted my teeth, struggling to keep it together. "I'll be gone one day and you'll be alone."

"Don't say it again, Cooper. I don't want someone else." Defiance in her eyes. "Stop feeling sorry for yourself."

"I'm not. You're the one I feel sorry for."

"Well, don't. Okay? Just don't."

I slid my arms up to her waist, her tiny waist. Had she always been so small? And I pulled her closer, her head resting on my shoulder, her body shaking with gentle sobs. I hated making her cry. Detested it. Despised myself because I wanted to make her happy and I was failing dismally.

She nudged me away. "Oh, I nearly forgot to tell you." She reached down, searching her purse for a few moments before coming up with a small container in her hand and a big smile on her face. "Halmoni sent you some of her special kim chi. Health giving, she said."

"And who am I to argue?"

I didn't have the heart to tell her I wasn't the world's biggest fan of the stuff.

Cupping Ginger's face in my hands, I pressed my lips to hers and kissed her, slowly at first, then deeper, longer. She always made me want more. All of her. Because simply being friends would never be enough.

She gave me hope, reminded me of something else the doctor had said. There'd been talk of new experimental drugs and treatments, but after two years with AIH, I'd given up believing in miracles.

This was where Ginger was a problem. She made me believe in miracles.

But they didn't exist. God knows I didn't want to die, didn't deserve this shit. No one did.

"I have to go now." Ginger stood. "But I'll be back later."

I kissed her like it was the last time because you never knew when that might come. And I'd rather she remembered the passion of our kiss than the wreck of a man before her.

"See you, Cooper." She turned and left.

I closed the door behind her.

"I love you, Ginger," I whispered.

My back pressed against the door, my chest lurching, body convulsing, I choked out the sobs I'd been holding back. I let it all go, tears streaming, nose running.

How could it hurt so much? Like my lungs had been punctured and my heart ripped from my chest. How could it have come to this?

My legs folding beneath me, I slid to the floor and slumped against the door like a crumpled mess.

Life was such a bitch. And death… Death would be worse for those who loved me.

How could I do this to Ginger? How?

CHAPTER FOURTEEN

Ginger

No way would Cooper miss the re-opening of The Swamp, not now that he was out of the hospital. He'd been living with auto-immune hepatitis for a couple of years and wouldn't let a little thing like that get in his way.

I still had trouble getting it through my head that he could be so ill and have so few symptoms. Except for vomiting blood at Morgan's party. That hadn't been little.

Maybe I was in denial. Maybe I'd wake up and find it had all been a bad dream. Maybe this would all go away.

But right now I had Cooper, his friends, and The Swamp. And I was clinging to these things.

"You've done an amazing job," I said to Nick.

"You're talking to the wrong man." He pulled Austin closer. "He's the genius behind this place."

I looked at Austin, their old bass player, now a full-time architect. "This place looks awesome."

He smiled. "Thanks."

I had no clue how he'd done it. The Swamp still had the air of a dive bar about it—that's what the place had always been—yet it'd been rearranged and cleaned up and revitalized. The same vibe, still with a grungy feel, but different. Dark but not dirty. And a hell of a lot better.

Before his wedding, Nick had asked me to take some 'before' shots of The Swamp so I'd seen the grime and dirt in more detail than I'd wanted.

Since then, they'd repositioned the bar and polished the wood, leaving the initials people had dug in at one spot, almost like an architectural relic. Behind the bar, bottles of liquor gleamed on sparkling glass shelves. A decent sized crowd milled around the tables and chairs, while some had settled into the booths along one wall.

Cooper whacked Austin on the shoulder. "I agree with Ginger. This is fucking awesome. You don't need us after all."

Austin spread his arms. "I'll always need my friends. That's never going to change."

Nick nudged him. "Enough about you. There's also Tara." Nick motioned to the bar. "I couldn't run this place without her."

And I couldn't miss the bar manager with the red lipstick and rockabilly styling, a purple streak in her hair. She and Austin made the perfect couple.

Lachie and Joel came up and greeted us, making me realize the whole band was in the one spot, old members and new. I pulled the Lumix out of my purse and wandered around the group, taking a few candid shots of them talking and laughing, people moving behind them, blurry figures in the foreground to give the pictures some depth. Natural shots.

One day, there'd be another member too, a new drummer. Cooper had told me they were looking for a replacement.

I swallowed back my anxiety even though I knew this was the way it had to be, then forced a smile to my face as Cooper approached me. Spotting a champagne glass in his hand, I did a double take.

He motioned for me to come closer, holding the glass out to me. "For you."

I relaxed, took a sip. "Sorry, I couldn't work out what was going on."

"I didn't want to disturb you, that was all. And I didn't want you to miss out."

Another sip. "How can I be missing out if I'm with you?"

His hand on my waist, he pressed a kiss to my cheek, making me feel small. My breath caught in my throat. I should make the most of every moment together even in a room full of people.

Nick stepped over. "That reminds me. I'd like you to take some 'after' shots of the bar. I'll give you a call about it."

"Sure."

He got pulled away by someone wanting to talk to him.

Jess came across, greeting us both with a kiss on the cheek, then looked down at the camera around my neck. "Are you going to be taking photos all night or are you going to have a good time?"

I held up my glass. "The latter, I think." I looked behind her. "Hanging out with Lily and Scarlett again?"

"Wedding talk," she said.

My eyes widened. What had I missed?

Jess laughed. "Not mine! Scarlett's getting married but she and Joel haven't set a date and she has no idea what sort of wedding she wants."

I hadn't seen much of her lately so I hoped she didn't feel left out. I'd barely seen much of anybody. Except Cooper. And most of the time I didn't want to see anyone else.

"It's amazing," Jess said. "Cooper looks so much better."

"Yeah, he does."

For now. My heart clenched, fear and yearning simmering in my stomach. This was too much for me, too much for Cooper, too much for anyone.

"Guess I should put this away." I slid the strap of the Lumix over my head and fiddled around as I put it away in my purse.

My Lumix, the same camera I'd used that night at Morgan's. I hadn't been able to look at the photos from the party, the guys playing that gig, not with what had happened that night.

Instead I'd downloaded the images of Cooper's family onto my computer because those pictures captured a special moment for Amy. And deleted everything else from the memory card. I had the only photos that mattered.

"Speech, speech."

I looked around, not sure who was yelling this out. None of the guys from the band obviously because Nick had said he wasn't giving any speeches.

"Speech, speech." Followed by some foot stamping.

Nick looked sheepish but the noise only got louder. He started waving his hands for them to stop but it didn't work.

Eventually, he yelled, "I'm done with speeches, guys!

We're here to party so have a drink and enjoy."

The crowd settled down after that. It still niggled—not the speeches but the other stuff that wasn't happening tonight, the things we were missing and that would never be right.

Taking a deep breath, I knocked back the rest of my champagne and walked across to place the empty glass on the bar. Cooper must've wandered off to talk to someone.

Then I spotted him wandering into the band room. On his own. The doors to that room were open but everyone had gathered in the main bar where the booze and the action were centered.

Something in the slope of his shoulders and the shuffle of his steps filled my stomach with sorrow. How could he look so sad from behind?

I followed and stood in the doorway of the band room, staring at Cooper like I was looking at life through a lens. As if this was a scene from a movie. As if we could switch this off and get back to the safety of our lives.

Safe … never again.

This was The Swamp, and that was how I felt. Swamped. Trudging through a quagmire. Always struggling.

His hands in his pockets, Cooper stood to one side, contemplating the mural that took up most of one wall. I'd seen Joel's enormous artwork before. Black and white with silver highlights, the mural showed Frankston's rock history, the bands who'd played here, the people, some I recognized, some I didn't.

Of course The Merchants were featured prominently on the wall. They'd been planning on performing a short set tonight. Until Morgan's party happened. After that

Nick had played it cool, insisting on no speeches, no band, that he was keeping the event simple.

Because the memory of Cooper spewing blood was too much for them. I understood that. My gut wrenched at the thought of it. But I wanted more for Cooper. I wanted to give him what he couldn't have.

And the band meant everything to him. His dreams had come true when they'd taken him on. The Merchants had been his whole life. And he never complained about this loss, this enormous change in his life. Didn't want to hold the other guys back.

I stared at my beautiful boyfriend. Despite the faces painted on the mural, despite the people in the next room, the guys from the band, people who loved him. Despite all this, Cooper looked so alone.

Dread hung over me like a shroud because I had a horrible feeling nothing I could do would change that.

CHAPTER FIFTEEN

Cooper

The imagery from the mural soaked into me, deep into my gut, much deeper than before. I'd seen the wall after it'd been finished but now I was viewing it with fresh eyes.

I stared at it with the eyes that'd been in the hospital after losing a truckload of blood, eyes that'd seen a dear friend withering from hepatitis, the eyes of a man whose sister was having a baby. Because no matter what happened, life went on. Other lives.

"Impressive, isn't it?" Ginger's voice. "You must've seen it before."

I turned to her. "Yeah, I have."

Fresh eyes, old eyes, all the things I should have paid attention to sooner. I'd seen Ginger with Thomas at Nick and Lily's wedding, and with the teenagers when she was taking photos at my old high school. I'd seen how happy she was for Amy even though she'd only just met her.

Ginger was made to have kids, maybe not today, maybe not even next year, but one day soon. It wasn't the sort of thing she should leave till she was forty and then hope for the best.

How could I have made such a mess of things? I'd married Lucy in Vegas because it'd seemed like a good idea at the time. I'd been a shit of a husband and a shit of a son. I was older now, smarter, more experienced, a better person.

And I couldn't do that to Ginger. A pang shot through my chest at the pain I was causing, the life I was ruining, the lie I was living.

I turned back to the mural. "Sometimes I wish I had a passion like this to fall back on, that I could create an artwork or design buildings or write a book."

She came closer. "You could take up art if you wanted to."

"Ha! You clearly haven't seen my drawings. My parents still have some pictures I did when I was eight. I haven't progressed since then."

"Everyone's got to start somewhere."

Which was exactly what I was doing. I'd lined up a meeting with a guy at Frankston University who seemed very interested in my idea of a scholarship. I might not be able to create an artwork but I could still leave something to the town.

I took her hand into mine. "You're always so positive."

"Yep."

This, from a woman who'd already had enough shit in her life to last a lifetime. She didn't need anymore. Despair flooded my heart.

I squeezed her hand, distraught because there'd come a time I wouldn't be able to do this. "I'm tired, Ginger, exhausted."

"Sure. We'll say goodbye to Nick and the others and

get going."

"No, let's just go. The quicker, the better. I can't handle it otherwise."

She didn't argue and we left swiftly.

Ginger buckled up in the car. "Sure you're all right to drive?"

"Believe me, I wouldn't drive if I wasn't fine. I learned my lesson years ago."

"Then what are we waiting for?"

For a miracle. I switched on the engine.

The cirrhosis diagnosis brought everything home, made death feel so much closer, so much more real. I had another appointment coming up with the gastroenterologist to discuss some new drugs. For what it was worth.

I drove, kept my eyes on the road, concentrated on what I was doing. Ginger talked about the evening and the people she'd spoken to. Not too much chat, just enough.

I pulled up outside her place, held her hand as we wandered to her apartment without speaking. Silence was okay too.

Inside, I asked for a glass of water while she made herself a peppermint tea. Always so considerate. If we were a normal couple, we'd be sharing a bottle of wine or at the very least she should be having a gin and tonic. She should be enjoying herself.

On the sofa, she pushed away her mug, turning to stare at me. "Sometimes I want all of you. I want to drink you all in."

"You're so serious all of a sudden."

"Not serious. Something else."

This was how I wanted to remember her, sometimes

deliberate and thoughtful, other times playful and petite, always attentive. Always Ginger.

Nuzzling into my neck, she pulled up my shirt, slid her hands onto the bare skin, then popped open the button on my jeans.

God, how I wanted this, but one of us had to be strong. I had to do the right thing. I covered her hand with mine, pushing it away from my crotch.

"What's up?" she asked.

Close, so close. I breathed her in, let her settle in my lungs, wishing I could always hold her near.

"Ginger, can you kiss me like you mean it?"

Like it's our last time, the words I didn't say.

She tilted her head. "I always kiss you like I mean it."

Her lips found mine. She tasted like peppermint and champagne, like home, like everything I'd ever wanted. Longing curled in my stomach. Longing for forever. She'd always stay in my heart.

Her fingers wandered to my crotch, and desire coursed through me. Desperation too.

I pulled her hand away. "I can't do this anymore, Ginger."

She frowned, then settled back into the sofa. "That's okay. We don't have to if you don't feel like it. We can just lie together tonight. It doesn't always have to be about sex."

"No, you don't understand. I'm talking about me and you."

"Me and you, what?"

"We have to break up. It's over, Ginger."

Lips parted, her face clouded over, and she edged back. Only an inch but I felt the distance.

I held my ground. "I'm sorry."

She scoffed, spluttered, couldn't quite get the words out.

"You deserve much better than I can give," I said.

"Says who?" She got the words out just fine now. "Damn it, Cooper, I can work out what's going on. You've still got some good years ahead of you."

"They won't all be good."

I'd had so few symptoms now—other than vomiting blood, quite a doozy—that Ginger probably found it hard to believe how bad things would get. But I'd seen what happened near the end, and Dave hadn't even made it to the worst part.

There was no avoiding death. For me, it'd be over one day regardless of whether it was quick or slow. A different story for my parents and family. They'd suffer more than me. Longer. Harder. No way around that either.

But I could stop Ginger from having to go through it. I could do this one honorable thing.

I sucked in a deep breath, stayed strong. "I've given this a lot of thought. It's better if we finish things now. I wish there was another way but there isn't."

Fire in her eyes, she pushed me away. "You are so wrong, Cooper."

Angry now. Angry was good. Maybe that'd make it easier for her.

"It's better this way," I said. "You'll find a nice guy, get married, have kids and a normal life."

Her eyes blazed with rage. "I don't want some other guy. What if we stayed together? What'd be so bad about that? Forget about having a child together. Maybe we'd have one, maybe we wouldn't. We'd work it out one way or another."

"You want children, Ginger. There's no denying it. I'll die one day soon and you'd still be young with a little kid on your hands. You'd be on your own, all alone, when that wasn't what you signed up for."

"Jesus, Cooper. I'd be a single mom. Worse things could happen. I've got family, friends, people who care for me. If it came to that, I'd have your parents too. I'd never be alone."

"You don't get it, Ginger. You'd have to watch me die. A long, slow, painful death. Forget about the crap doctors come out with about making me 'comfortable'. Death is death. And you'd never feel more alone that you would then. And afterward. Afterward is a long time."

She threw her hands up. "Why are we even talking about this? We can still be together, children or no children. I haven't had a chance to think that part through. I mean, was I supposed to have had my life mapped out already?"

"You can't imagine going through life without having children. You already told me that, not that you needed to. I could see it in your eyes."

Her body shook, tears tumbling down her cheeks. "You know what I can't imagine?" Her voice cracked. "I can't imagine going through life without *you*."

I leaned forward, my arms resting on my thighs. "That's the whole point. You won't need to imagine it. You'd be going through it. There'd be no escape."

She edged forward, bumping my leg to make sure she had my attention. "It's not fair, Cooper."

"I know it isn't."

"That's not what I meant. This is my life we're talking

about too. You don't get to decide for me. What makes you think you're so smart, that you know what's best? For me? Because this is me we're talking about too." She gritted her teeth through the tears. "It's not your decision."

I stayed strong, held her gaze and shook my head. I wasn't going to tell her that one day she'd come to see this was the right decision for both of us, that I had to hurt her now to save her immeasurable pain in the future. Too condescending, too simplistic, and that wasn't how I saw it.

Or how I felt it. Because right now my heart was being ripped from my chest, my gut twisting, my throat tight. How much more could a man take?

"What about a liver transplant?" Her eyes hooded over. "Drugs, treatment, something."

"There's no cure, Ginger. That's the one thing I've always known."

I gazed at her. I'd done this to her. Shoulders scrunched, hands balled into fists, her tearstained face waxy with desperation. Still, this was better than staying with her and forcing her to suffer even more.

"I love you, Cooper," she spluttered, her body shaking. "I was too scared to tell you before."

"I love you too, Ginger."

That was what made this so hard. Also why I had to do this.

I pulled her sobbing body close to mine and held her. For now. She'd be alone soon enough.

CHAPTER SIXTEEN

Ginger

Maybe this was one of the reasons Cooper had wanted to make sure I didn't let my work slip. Maybe he'd known all along that he was going to break up with me. And break my heart in the process, shatter it into a thousand pieces, cut me to the core.

Studio, job, client, concentrate.

I examined the test shot on the back of the camera. "Stay there, I just need to shift the light a little."

The woman remained perched on a stool in front of the white backdrop. She was starting up her own cupcake business and had specified a white background so her graphic designer could deep etch the image into some brochures.

I stepped back to the camera. "Have you always liked to bake?"

She nodded. "Always."

"So how did you get started?"

Such a relief to listen to her chat about her beginnings, so much easier than when I was talking, forcing myself to act normal, swallowing back the pain I carried with me. It gave me the time to adjust the aperture and take another test shot.

"Okay, nearly ready," I said. "I'll count you in. One, two, three."

She gave a wan smile.

"Come on, you can do better than that." I pulled a face, forcing myself to ham it up to make her relax. "Think about cupcakes. Think about the way you pipe the icing in those cute roses. Think about red velvet, my favorite."

"Mine too."

She brightened and I took a series of good shots. She'd have to be happy with these. I called her over to show her the images on the back of the camera.

Her smile grew wider. "Wow, I don't normally like having my photo taken but these look great."

"Awesome. I'll email you a Dropbox link with the photos."

Yep, a girl still had to make a living, broken heart or not, the one thing Cooper had been right about.

Cooper. A pang shot through my chest. It hurt to say his name, even in my head.

I cleared my throat. "I'll see you to the door."

Outside, I walked her to the end of the front path outside my parents' house. The sun still had a bite to it even though it was getting late in the day. A short walk, a bit of vitamin D, a spot of sunshine, all things that should make me feel better. Instead I struggled with the simplest of things.

As soon as my client slammed her car door shut, Mom came out of the house. She'd probably been listening out for this, wanting to keep an eye on me. She'd been doing a lot of that lately.

She waved. "Why don't you come in for a coffee, honey?"

I headed back up the front path. "I'd love to, but I have heap of processing and computer work to do, still from yesterday's job."

"It's wonderful you've got so much work."

Yep, at least one thing was going well for me.

I pulled open the studio door. "We can chat while I pack up my camera bag. How was work today?"

Mom's mouth twisted. "I don't like seeing you like this."

I stood by the table with my gear on it, dredging up a smile designed to make her feel better. "I'll be fine, Mom. I can't expect to get over this in an instant. It's going to take time."

"You've always done your own thing."

I took the flash sync off the camera and removed the lens hood. "You say that like it's a bad thing."

"I used to think it was." She slumped down in a nearby chair. "I was so upset when you ran away from home."

As a nice Korean girl, I'd been expected to stay at home until I got married. So different from Alistair, a good Korean boy who'd done the right thing by waiting till he was married to leave home.

I couldn't deal with this now, not on top of the dread that was weighing me down, the constant knot in my stomach, the loss I carried with me. But I had enough fight in me to keep going.

"Mom, I was twenty. I had a job and I moved out."

"You're not like Alistair. In so many ways, you're a better person than him."

"Sorry?"

Had I heard right? My head started spinning.

She said, "Alistair's very clever in lots of ways but he's not nearly as sensitive or caring as you. So often he's thinking about himself whereas you're much more aware of others."

Still in shock, I placed my gear in the camera bag and secured the flap. "Thank you."

"It ripped me up when you quit college and moved out of our home and did everything you weren't supposed to."

"Come on, Mom, it's not as if I was some criminal living on the streets."

She got up and wandered closer. "No, but it felt that way at the time. To me, anyway. Your father was more understanding."

We were back to this again. My stomach dropped, anger and anxiety simmering deep inside. I didn't even know what I was feeling anymore.

"I let you down," I spat the words out. "I was always letting you down."

"Not at all, honey. That's what I'm trying to tell you. My reactions weren't about you. They were about *me*. Dad was born here and has found his place in the world, whereas I've always been stuck between two cultures, pulled in both directions, a grown woman in the midst of an identity crisis. Am I American? Am I Korean? I don't always know the answer. Maybe I took that out on you."

"I could never be the person you wanted me to be," I said, my voice shaking.

Mom reached for my fingers, took my hand into hers. "And I finally worked out you didn't need to be. That it wasn't fair, that it would never make you happy."

My lower lip trembled. "Unfortunately it hasn't worked. I'm not very happy at the moment."

Understatement of the year. For all intents and purposes, I functioned. I looked like a normal person, but my heart had been broken so many times there was no fixing it. No cure, no solution, no way I could take anymore.

Mom squeezed my hand. "I'm sorry about how things have worked out with Cooper. As a mother, I can't say it was my dream for you to find a young man who was dying. No parent wants that for their child. At the same time, it wasn't that much of a surprise to me that you'd care for someone no matter what."

"Well, it was a shock to me when I found out."

"You're such a wonderful young woman, honey, and I'd like to see that spark in your eye again, that girl who does things her way, because you were always true to yourself. I just didn't see it sooner."

"I really appreciate this." My voice was small, the emotion inside me huge, my chest swelling.

"I don't know exactly where you're headed, honey. I only know that you'll get there."

We held each other close and I let the tears fall, tears of gratitude, of fear for the future, tears for a miracle that wasn't going to happen.

CHAPTER SEVENTEEN

Cooper

The doctor sat opposite me behind his desk, an ordinary looking guy in his fifties wearing an open necked shirt, but there was nothing everyday about what he was saying.

He leaned forward, his hands together, fingers intertwined. "I need to make it clear that USTR is not a miracle drug. Like all drugs, there are side effects and other repercussions."

"Yes." I'd taken enough medication to know that. It was a question of how good the results would be and whether the benefits outweighed the risks.

"There's no cure for AIH or cirrhosis. That hasn't changed. USTR works by protecting the existing healthy liver tissue and preventing further scarring from occurring."

His words should have been reassuring but my gut was clenched in fear—that this was too good to be true, that he might have got it wrong, that this was another one of life's cruel tricks.

I swallowed back my anxiety and nodded for him to continue.

"It's about maintenance. The idea is to keep things at the same level for as long as we can, for years hopefully. Treatment is still partially experimental. You'd be among the first people who are administered the drug outside the early trials."

Did I dare to believe? Did I dare to think about Ginger, the pain I'd caused, the pain that still lay within me?

"This is incredible," I choked out the words. "It's ... a second chance."

"Not quite. Sorry, but I need to make sure you understand this isn't an answer to all your problems. There's no permanent solution. Our aim is to extend your life for as long as we can, possibly for decades. Eventually the liver will build up immunity to USTR and when that happens, you'll start to decline again. At that point, we will have exhausted all possibilities, other than that of a liver transplant, but that's another story."

I gritted my teeth. He'd been through this with me before. My situation would need to be dire—near death—to be considered for a liver transplant and even then, I wouldn't make it to old age. Nowhere near it.

Yet now he was telling me I'd most likely have many years ahead of me, good years, not years of terrible health and struggling to get out of bed. Decades, that was the word he'd used.

I'd die younger than most people, but until then I'd have a life. I'd have time, the one thing I didn't have before.

My throat tight, my whole body on edge, trepidation thrummed inside my chest. I wanted to believe, wanted this to be true, but the last two years had been filled with such disappointment and devastating news that I couldn't bear another blow, not if this didn't work out.

"It's lucky you're a good candidate," the doctor said. "Because of your age, your physical condition, your lifestyle, the way you take care of yourself and follow doctors' instructions diligently."

"I'm diligent, all right!"

Hadn't always been that way. Had been the complete opposite in fact. A selfish prick if I was going to be honest. Yet another reason for me to be anxious.

The doctor ushered me out of his office. He was always running behind schedule and I didn't care. I was going to live—for a while anyway—if what he'd said was true, if the drug worked, if things worked the way he'd described.

I drove to The Swamp in a daze, a careful daze where I kept an eye on the traffic, following all the rules and paying attention to the traffic because that's the kind of person I was. Diligent. It made me smile. A few years ago, I wouldn't even have considered that a compliment.

The Swamp looked better than it had the last time I'd been here. The only people hanging around in the middle of the afternoon were a few tourists and a couple of old guys who looked like they were glued to the bar. Previous patrons. Good for them if they still liked the place.

Nick waved to me from the bar so I wandered across, admiring the new stools—red leather and free of rips— and the bar in its polished wood glory. Everything seemed clearer in daylight, the world brighter. Maybe the news was starting to sink in, after all.

"Hi, Tara," I said to the bar manager.

"Nice to see you." She raised her eyebrows. "Two

mineral waters?"

"Thanks." I turned to Nick. "Since when are you drinking water?"

"Since it's the middle of the afternoon." He took the glass she handed him, passed one across to me, motioning for me to join him at a table. "Also since Tara told me to clean up my act."

"I must've missed that."

He motioned for me to join him at a table. "I wouldn't worry. You haven't missed much."

I sat opposite him, facing the bar, the door to my left.

Nick stared at me. "You look good, better than you have in a while."

"Ah, thanks."

Should I tell him what the doctor had said? No, I wanted to tell my family first.

And Ginger.

My stomach sank because there was no Ginger anymore, not like that. There was only the space where she had once been, the hole she'd left, the pain that ripped through my heart whenever I thought of her.

I rubbed my chin. "Man, I've had a day of appointments, from one to the other."

"What's up?"

"First, I met that guy from Frankston University, the one I told you about, to discuss scholarships. Didn't go so well. He was all about the money. That was the only thing he was interested in. He just didn't get it."

"So what did you do?"

"I hadn't even made it off campus when I was phoning Catherine, the principal from Wilson High."

Nick whooped. "You? On first name terms with the

school principal? Hilarious."

"I know. Scary thing is, she was on the same wavelength as me. She could see where I was coming from and that I wanted to help. Her idea is for a scholarship scheme administered by the school to help selected students go to the college of their dreams, tuition and living costs, so they can study wherever they want. We still need to iron out the finer details but I said I'd like to help the kids who most need it, those from poor backgrounds or who have an illness."

I brimmed with satisfaction at the thought. I'd had no idea something like this could feel so good. No strings, no expectation of anything in return, but it felt as if some of that good karma was coming my way.

Nick leaned back in his chair. "Ah, the Cooper McVeigh Scholarship Scheme. Who would've thought?"

"Hang on, I won't be naming it after myself. Maybe I'll call it Snare or Cymbals. Hey, maybe I'll spell it S-Y-M-B-O-L like it's a symbol of something else."

He nodded. "So deep."

I laughed. "I try."

I still had to speak to my accountant about setting up a trust for the scholarship, something to give it longevity because I wanted this to go on for decades.

Like *I* might go on for decades, or maybe that was wishful thinking. Still, it was a possibility, not a dream, not anymore. My throat tightened. This was a day of ups and downs, a day of mixed feelings.

The two old guys staggered away from the bar, not glued to it after all. They stepped away from the door when they reached it, making way for someone, one of them bowing in an exaggerated move.

Ginger, stepping through the doorway, thanked the two old guys for making way, smiling as if they'd done her a huge favor.

A pang shot through my chest. So kind, so gentle, so everything I'd ever wanted. What a huge mistake I'd made. The pain I'd caused. The agony I kept locked inside me.

Finally, I could see what was right before my eyes.

Such a slender thing, her figure outlined in fitted pants and a tight tee, one shoulder was weighed down from her camera bag. Which only showed how strong she was. Stronger than I'd given her credit for.

She spotted me and stopped, her lips parting. Then her mouth set with determination as she strode toward our table.

I stood. Nick stepped forward to give her a quick kiss on the cheek, looking sheepish and as guilty as I'd ever seen him. What a set-up. I could tell from the look on Ginger's face that she had no idea I'd be here.

"Hi, Nick." She held a hand out to me. "No need to stand."

A bit late since I was already on my feet. I held my feelings in check, refused to take this as a rebuttal.

I pointed to her camera bag. "Can I take that for you? Do you need a hand?"

"No thanks. It's nothing I haven't lugged around a hundred times before." She held my gaze, staring deep into my eyes. "How are you doing, Cooper?"

"I'm fine."

She shook her head. "No, I mean, how are you doing, really?"

Did that mean she cared? Did she still love me? My throat dry, I swallowed back the apprehension simmering inside.

"My condition's stable, if that's what you mean."

"Well, that's … good."

"How are you, Ginger?"

"Busy. I'd better hop to it." She turned to Nick. "I'll start in the band room."

This is what we were reduced to—polite inquiries into each other's health, not even small talk before she made her escape. I watched her leave, regret reverberating through my body with each step she took before she disappeared from sight.

I sat down again, my head in my hands. "What were you thinking, Nick?"

He shrugged. "I need Ginger to take documentary photos of the place."

"No kidding."

"And I need to talk to you too."

"No shit."

"No, really. We've been skirting around the issue, me and the other guys, but we were wondering if you'd be up to playing The Flats?"

Another of my dreams, a dream that still took my breath away, not something I could give up, especially since I might never get another chance. But I couldn't screw everything up for my friends, couldn't let them down again. Desperation coiled inside me.

"I gotta be honest," I said. "You can't rely on me to get through a one-hour set."

He raised his eyebrows. "But you could do a few songs? Half a dozen? Whatever we decide on."

"You'd like that?"

Nick grinned. "Are you kidding? We'd love to have

you on that stage with us. We were thinking you could pick the songs you wanted to play and we'd get the new guy to do the rest."

I heaved a sigh of relief. "That'd be absolutely fucking awesome."

"Now all we've got to do is decide on the new guy."

"Good luck," I said.

He glanced toward the band room. "You too."

Taking a deep breath, I stood and walked away. Ginger had pulled the doors to the band room closed behind her so I knocked before walking in.

The size of the stage made her look small as she sat on the edge, camera in hand, looking out.

"Are you okay?" I asked.

"Yeah, I'm just trying to get a different perspective. Imagining the vibe, this place full of people, wondering what it's like to play on stage."

"I can answer that." I sat beside her on the stage. "It's a rush, a fantastic feeling. When everything clicks, it's like we're swept up in a wave, part of an irresistible force that's bigger than any of us. There's nothing else quite like it. Better than drugs, better than booze. Because it's real."

Real, like her. Anguish gripped me, tearing me up from the inside out, only it had nothing to do with the band and everything to do with the woman sitting beside me on stage. So close I could reach out and touch her, except I didn't dare ruin the moment. And I didn't have the right to touch her anymore.

"Your photos capture that feeling," I said. "They're loaded with emotion."

"Thanks. It means a lot to me for you to say that."

"How are you doing with images for your book? Do

you have enough?"

"It's never enough." She smiled. "I want to get some shots at The Flats Festival to round things out."

"Sure."

"And I've been talking to the publishers at Frankston Press and also to their guy who does the layout. So things for the book are well underway."

"That's excellent."

I told her how I'd spoken to Catherine at Wilson High and the idea of creating a trust to take care of the scholarship. I asked about her family. Anyone who saw us would probably think we were having a normal conversation, but there was nothing normal about the way I felt, the tugging in my heart, the tension in my chest.

"How's Amy?" Ginger asked.

"Same as the last time you saw her. No morning sickness but she's tired all the time. Excited. Happy. Over the moon."

"I saw her the other day. When I dropped off a USB with the images for her."

"I know."

Yep, my sister was having a baby, a new life being created, a new day dawning. It made me think about what I wanted from life, however long or short that life might be. Made me think about what I've always wanted and what was important.

No matter which direction I went or which subject I was thinking about, somehow it always came back to Ginger.

And after my appointment with the specialist this morning, I had hope. Everyone needed a little hope.

She stood, camera in hand. "I'd better get on with it."

I looked up at her. "There's something I have to tell you."

"Not now, Cooper."

Standing up to join her, I looked into her eyes. Tired. I'd pushed her to extremes. Guilt flooded me. I'd done this to the person I loved most in the world.

"Another time then," I said. "We can have a drink, a coffee, something."

She gave a curt shake of her head. "You broke my heart, Cooper."

And my own in the process. I hated seeing her like this, the pain in her eyes, the truth of her words. It cut deep. Made me gasp.

I backed off slowly, holding her gaze, then turned and left her to it. I knew exactly what I had to do, and the first thing involved changing out of jeans and a T-shirt.

Hope. Just a glimmer, that was all I needed.

CHAPTER EIGHTEEN

Ginger

I pulled open the front door, my breath catching in my throat. "Cooper, what are you doing here?"

"Visiting you."

Leaning my head against the door, I pressed my eyes shut for a moment. How could he do this? I didn't blame him for our encounter at The Swamp yesterday. That had Nick's name written all over it. I'd tried to have a regular conversation with Cooper but I couldn't do it. We could never be friends.

Before I knew it, he walked through the door and onto the landing that led to my living room. I needed a bigger apartment, one with a hallway so he wouldn't be in the middle of my home already.

"You can't stay," I said.

"But you invited me in."

My mouth fell open. "No, I didn't."

He edged closer, as serious as I'd ever seen him. "I need to talk to you, Ginger."

Damn it, Cooper, you are everything I need and the last thing I need is to talk to you.

I gritted my teeth. "This is too painful. Seeing you yesterday threw me. I wasn't expecting it and maybe if I had been, it might've made it easer for me. You can't just show up on my doorstep and expect us to have a normal relationship. There's no 'normal' for me and you anymore."

"Have you finished?"

I balled my hand into a fist. "I haven't even started. I've got a book to produce and a career to focus on and a thousand things to do." I glared at him. "All those things I didn't do because I was spending all my time with you, well, all those things are waiting to be done."

"You're cute when you ramble."

I wanted to hit him, but he melted my heart a little, a smidgen, just enough. No, I had to stand up for myself.

"You can't say things like that to me," I said. "You're not my boyfriend anymore."

His lips parted. "I'm sorry. You're right about that. Ginger, can I have just ten minutes of your time please? Surely that's not too much to ask, not when I'm here already."

I pressed my lips together to stop them trembling. "Okay, ten minutes." I pointed to the sofa. "Then you have to go."

"Deal."

He sat at one end of the sofa, placing a brown paper bag with raffia handles at his feet. I hoped he hadn't bought me a present. Hoped he didn't think he could fix this with money and gifts. Disgust curdled in my stomach.

"I saw the gastroenterologist yesterday," he said.

I dropped down onto the sofa. Hadn't seen this coming. What could the doctor possibly have had to say after everything Cooper had been through?

If I could click my fingers and change one thing, I'd give him a clean bill of health. Didn't matter if we were together or not. Didn't matter that it felt as if my heart had been yanked from my chest. As long as Cooper kept breathing.

He told me about a new drug, a game changer, he called it. Not a cure. There'd never be one of those.

"I can't lie to you," he said. "AIH will still kill me. The cirrhosis can only be held at bay for so long. The end will still be terrible. When it comes. But it's far enough away that I can focus now. I've got more time, maybe even decades, and I've got hope."

Tears sprang from my eyes, tumbling down my cheeks. I covered my mouth, tried to stop myself from shaking, waiting till the tremors in my heart died down.

"You'll live," I spluttered.

He nodded. "For a while."

Throwing my arms around him, I let him pull me close as he rubbed my back until I stopped trembling. The tears stopped too, and eventually I pulled back, Cooper's hands gripping mine as they lay on his knees.

"I got you something." He reached into the bag at his feet, handing me a Merchants of Menace T-shirt. In Korean.

I held it out, a big smile on my face. "It's perfect."

Placing it on the arm of the chair behind me, I turned to find Cooper looking at me. Waiting.

"We're all dying, Ginger, and I'm no different. I'm just going to do it sooner than the rest of you. I've come to a realization. I'm here to live. My life, my way. With you."

Could it be true? My chest tightened, the air leaving my body.

He slid closer. "When I thought I only had a few years left, I couldn't do that to you. Couldn't put you through that agony, only to leave you so soon." He paused. "I can give you more now. And more than anything, I want to give you all my love."

He slipped his hand into the bag again, came up with a small velvet box. And got down on one knee.

"Ginger, will you marry me?"

A proposal … after everything we'd been through? This couldn't be happening. I opened my mouth but no words came out.

He took my hand into his. "The commitment is the part that's important to me. It's not about the ring or the wedding. I want to give myself to you, everything that's left of me. I want to be there for you today and tomorrow and for as long as I'm here."

"Yes." My voice barely a croak, I tried again, louder this time. "Yes."

Cooper slipped the ring box into my hand, slid up to the sofa, and pressed his lips against mine. This kiss wouldn't be our last. It'd be the first. Of many.

Hands shaking, I opened the little box. And stared.

Then looked up at him. "It's empty."

"I thought you'd want to choose the ring yourself. After all, you're going to be wearing it every day and I didn't want to get the wrong one. I never even had the chance to suss out what sort of ring you'd like, gold, silver, diamonds, something else. I didn't even know where to start."

I laughed, covered my mouth to stop myself from

spluttering. "Lucky you already gave me the T-shirt or you'd be in big trouble."

He pulled me close. "I want you forever, and maybe forever will go on for longer than I think."

"I'm so happy, Cooper. I can't wait to tell my parents. Alistair too." I held out my hand as if showing off the ring. "They'll just have to use their imaginations."

"They already know."

My mouth fell open.

"I went to see your dad yesterday, your mom too," he said. "To ask for your hand in marriage because I wanted to do this properly."

I placed a hand on my chest. "I had no idea you were so old fashioned."

"Only when it comes to you." Cooper pressed a kiss to my lips, stayed close. "Let's have a baby together. Because I don't want to wait."

The truth? I didn't want to wait either. Waiting was for other people who had more time, who didn't know what they wanted, people who weren't us. Those darned tears started streaming down my face again.

"I want to throw a ball to my child," Cooper said. "And take him to the park and teach him how to bang on the drums."

"Hey." I nudged him away. "Who say's it'll be a boy? Girls can play the drums too, you know."

He laughed, such a beautiful sound. "I don't mind. A little girl who looked like you would be perfect too."

The doorbell rang, the sound making me jump.

"I nearly forgot," Cooper said. "That'll be the *crochembouche* cake."

My mouth dropped open. "What?"

"I thought if you tried to turn me down, that this might seal the deal."

I laughed. Couldn't believe it.

"We can take it to your parents' place." Cooper extricated himself from my grasp. "Or when we go to see my parents to give them the good news."

I smiled. "Halmoni will love it."

And so would I.

Maybe we wouldn't have forever but if I had Cooper, I'd have everything I ever wanted.

CHAPTER NINETEEN

Cooper

I stared at the instructions on the box. "You're a girl. Aren't you supposed to be good at this stuff?"

Ginger looked up at me, longing in her warm brown eyes. "I haven't done this before either."

"It says to dip the stick in a quarter inch of urine for five seconds."

"Okay."

I stared at her. "Well, what are you waiting for?"

She threw her hands up. "For some privacy. I can't just wee on demand."

"Why not?"

Her hands on my chest, she pushed me out of the bathroom and closed the door. Leaning against the wall, I gave her some time but not too much. I was impatient as all hell too.

According to the instructions on the box, the kit should be reliable one to two weeks after missing a period. Ginger hadn't so much as missed her last period, as not noticed it hadn't happened.

"Getting kicked out of the bathroom in my own

home!" I yelled through the door. "What's the world coming to?"

"*Your* home?" She pulled the door open and stuck her head through. "This is my home now too, you know."

"I know." I pressed a kiss to her cheek. "And I wouldn't have it any other way."

She closed the door. I gave her a moment.

"Have you done a wee yet?" I barged in to see the little cup sitting by the sink.

She sidled up next to me. "Yes, and I've got the stick."

I covered her hand with mine. "Your hand is shaking."

"I'm nervous. I told you, I haven't done this before."

"That makes two of us." I pressed a kiss to her cheek, pulled her close. "I don't want you to be upset if it's negative. There's always next time. Or the time after that. And in the meantime, we can just keep practicing."

"But I've got a feeling about this."

She'd been through this with me already. This 'feeling' didn't extend as far as morning sickness, sudden intolerances to certain foods, or any actual signs of pregnancy. It was a sign of her excitement, and that scared the hell out of me. I couldn't bear the thought of her disappointment if this didn't work out.

"Who's going to dip the stick in?" she asked. "Me or you?"

"You can do it."

"Okay."

"What are you waiting for?"

She scrunched up her pretty face. "What if it's negative?"

"Don't worry, Ginger. Not everyone gets pregnant the first time they try."

"I wasn't even trying to start with."

We'd been sloppy on our first night together, and it could've ended badly but it hadn't. We were together and that was all that mattered.

She sucked in a breath. "Okay, I'm ready."

"I'm sure it doesn't take other people this long." I couldn't keep the smile from my face.

One hand on her hip, she glared. "You're not taking this seriously."

"Of course, I am. I've never been more serious about anyone in my life than I am about you."

"Okay." She held the stick over the cup, steeling herself. "Here goes. One hippopotamus, two hippopotamus."

"What're you doing?"

"Counting. Three. Four. Five. Okay, I'll take it out now. The instructions said to count to five."

"It didn't say you had to count out loud."

"What difference does that make? It's not going to have any effect on the result."

She pouted. And I couldn't resist. I took the stick from her, placing it carefully on the counter, then wrapped my arms around her, covered her mouth with mine, and kissed her. Gently at first, then deeper, with more passion.

"Doesn't matter what happens," I said. "I love you."

"Love you too." She pressed a quick kiss to my lips and turned, stopping in her tracks. Didn't stay stopped for very long. Within a second, she was jumping up and down.

"We've got two pink lines." Still jumping, she slid an arm around my waist. "You know what that means."

I would've kissed her if she stayed still.

"We're going to have a baby," I said.

And nothing could have been more amazing.

Keep reading for a sneak preview of Book Six…

ACKNOWLEDGMENTS

First of all, a big thanks to my very own rock star and in-house consultant, James.

Thanks very much to the people I interviewed, all experts in your particular fields and very patient with my dumb questions—Jenny Kim, Brooke Lundy, Scott Wilson, Brendan Murphy and Jo Taylor. Thanks heaps, guys!

And of course thanks to my fabulous critique partners, Claire, Lorraine, Juanita, Teena and Anna.

ABOUT THE AUTHOR

Susanna Rogers is the author of rock star romances for adults and kick butt books for young adults. Inspired by her very own in-house rock star and years of going to gigs, she penned the Mosh Series after writing and releasing several young adult novels. She's also a kickboxer and dreams of empowering girls and guys around the globe to believe in themselves, to take care and follow their own dreams. She has a soft spot for romantic suspense, also with kick butt heroines, so you never know what might be coming up next.

She would love to hear from you—susannarogers.com.

If you like her books, please post a review on Amazon or Goodreads. She'd like that a lot.

GROUND & POUND
MOSH BOOK 6

CHAPTER ONE

Holly

Maybe Morgan had forgotten. After all, a person could forget a lot of things in four years.

He'd sure done well for himself. I'd kill for a kitchen like this, immaculate in white with a huge island counter, state-of-the-art stainless steel appliances, glass splash-backs, everything a home-chef could want.

And filled with people. Everyone wanted to be your friend when you were a successful record producer, everyone except me because the last thing I needed was a friend like him.

Tentative about talking to the host, I was hanging out in the kitchen, but had no clue why these others would be here when they could be lounging on the leather sofas or relaxing by the pool. So many options, so many rooms for that matter.

Out of nowhere, Morgan Masterson came striding toward the kitchen. Like a man on a mission. Like he owned the place.

Nerves raced through my body. There was no escaping that searing gaze. As he looked at me through lowered lids, I felt him peeling off my clothes with his eyes, layer by layer, imagining me naked, not that he'd have to try very hard because the memory might be imprinted in his mind.

I bit back my embarrassment, the memory of how stupid I'd been.

He stepped closer, his shoulders stiffening. Shit, I'd made a mistake, a big one. That was no seductive look. How could I have thought that for a second? I hoped like hell he wasn't going to kick me out or make a big deal of this.

He leaned against the counter, looking as suave as ever. "If it isn't Holly Jacobs."

I forced a smile. "Hey, Morgan."

"What brings you here tonight?"

"Oh, the same as everyone else. Happy Birthday."

I had to kiss him, so I made it quick. A peck on the cheek, nothing more but it was long enough for me to get a whiff of aftershave, something subtle and masculine. Typical.

"Thank you," he said.

"It's not every day a guy turns thirty."

He tried to blow a stray lock of hair out of his eyes, then raked a hand through to get the hair off his face, looking a lot like James Dean needing a haircut. Back when he was alive, that was.

"Thank you for reminding me," Morgan said.

"What? Thirty's not old."

He kept looking at me. I wished he wouldn't. I should keep talking, keep him distracted, then he might not realize he hadn't invited me, probably wouldn't even think about it.

"The top I'm wearing is probably thirty years old. From the eighties." Or maybe it was nineties. I really wouldn't know. I only knew what I liked, and I liked to throw different combinations of clothes together. The top was high-necked, fitted, fabulous, and went perfectly with my ripped jeans. I probably should've worn a bra, though.

"It suits you." He held my gaze, didn't look down at my chest, thank goodness.

Surely he wouldn't mind me being here. I was just as much a part of the Frankston music scene as anyone else here. I'd played the drums for years and had managed bands too. Well, one band. It had turned into a minor disaster, mostly because I hadn't known the first thing about the music industry at the time, but they'd been desperate and I'd helped. Besides you had to be a hard ass to be a band manager. I should've known that from the start.

"I got you something," I said.

"Very kind but there was really no need. It's not that sort of party."

"What sort is it?"

He shrugged. "The kind where everyone drinks a lot and has a good time."

"I can do that!"

A smile tugged at the corners of his lips. Maybe I was winning him over after all.

"I didn't want to come empty handed." I pointed to the corner where people had left a few gifts. "Mine's the one with the big red bow. I thought, what do you get the man who has everything?"

"That's kind of why the invitation said 'no gifts' because I'd rather people didn't waste their money when there are so many better things they can do with it."

An invitation, I didn't have one of those. Think quickly, Holly.

"Oh, I didn't waste any money on you."

He raised his eyebrows. "Really?"

My face flushed. "You didn't let me finish. I thought it'd be silly for me to try to guess what you might want so rather than head to the store, I baked some cookies."

"You baked me cookies." Surprise, followed by a sly look. "Sure they're not poisoned?"

I liked his teasing tone. Two could play at that game so I planted my hands on my hips. "It might not be too late for me to drizzle some arsenic on them. If they taste like almonds, you'll know why."

"What do almonds have to do with it?"

"Arsenic tastes like bitter almonds." He stared at me, so I added, "Or so I've been told. Don't you know anything?"

"Apparently not." He sidled closer, not a lot, only enough to stake his claim. "So you've been planning and plotting this?"

I held my ground. "Hey, they're cookies. I can take them back if you like."

"I wouldn't dream of it." His expression softened. "Not when you've done something so kind. My grandma used to bake cookies for me when I was little but I can't remember the last time that happened."

"Great, I remind you of your grandma."

The words slipped out the way they always did. Still, better I reminded him of his grandmother than a drunk nineteen-year-old girl who'd practically thrown herself at him four years ago. Maybe he had forgotten after all.

"My gran is a wonderful woman and a very good

cook."

"So am I." Yep, there I went, putting my foot in my mouth again. "I mean, I'm pretty good in the kitchen. Well, not that good really. I just like to cook."

"That's handy because most people like to eat." A pause, the uncomfortable kind, the kind that made me nervous, then he added. "Do you still play in the Maybe Dolls?"

"No, I'm between bands at the moment."

Between bands, between jobs, between homes. My life had become a huge 'in between' thanks to a combination of lousy circumstances. My roommate, Jess, had left our apartment to move in with Lachie, guitar player extraordinaire and a great guy to boot, absolutely the best thing that could have happened to her.

Not long after, the lease for the apartment had come up, and friends of my parents needed a house sitter while they were in Europe, someone to look after their plants and feed the fish. The timing had been too good. I couldn't argue with three months free rent, starting in a week.

Morgan cleared his throat as if he was about to make an announcement or maybe because I wasn't giving him enough attention.

He turned to me. "So did you come with someone tonight or did you crash the party on your own?"

Teasing was one thing but this was a bit close to the bone, even if I should be used to feeling unwanted.

"I didn't crash anything. I came with Jess and Lachie. Well, not *with* them exactly. They got here first."

Besides I had to be here to see The Merchants, my all-time favorite band, the sort of band I could only dream about playing with. They were playing a set later and no way could I miss them.

Drum and bass had been playing when I walked in. Now it was Post Malone. Morgan must have varied tastes.

"Great," he said. "I'm glad you didn't gatecrash."

"Absolutely not. I … wandered."

He burst out laughing. "You wandered. So you're a wanderer? Like a burglar, do they wander in too?"

I straightened. "The door was open."

"No, it wasn't."

"Okay, it was unlocked. Same thing."

He crossed his arms. "How'd you get past Bill?"

"Oh, I… We…"

I'd known Bill for ages, had met him doing security at gigs years ago, and then Jess and Lachie had come to the door after I'd texted to say I was outside. Lachie greeted me with a big hug, said they'd been waiting for me. Made getting in pretty easy.

Morgan gave me a dull look. "You sweet-talked him, then waltzed straight in, didn't you?"

Guilty as charged, not that I'd admit it. "I didn't *waltz* anywhere."

"Of course, you *wandered*. Hmm, I'll have to be more careful from now on."

I jabbed my finger at his folded arms and he dropped them.

"Look, I'm sorry if I came in uninvited—or if you hadn't invited me—but I didn't think it'd be so terrible for me to turn up."

"Who said it was terrible?"

Such a relief. "So you don't mind?"

"Not too much." He smiled. "I just thought you

might've messaged me or found some way of getting in touch. My website has a contact page. Or you could've asked Jess or Lachie. Lots of ways of reaching me."

Warmth settled inside me—at his gaze, his attention, at the fact he wanted me to call him. Maybe he'd forgotten I used to have his number, the one I'd deleted years ago. I could hope he'd forgotten all about that.

"Hey," I said. "I'm only one person. I'm not even that big."

He looked me up and down, an amused smile on his face. "Quite petite in fact."

"And I didn't think anyone would even notice me."

"I noticed you from the moment you first snuck in."

He gave me a look that was either admiring or admonishing, I couldn't tell which and had no clue where I stood with this guy. Or what I was supposed to do.

"I did not sneak. Besides, 'snuck' is not even a word. It's 'sneaked' and I didn't do that. I already told you that."

"That's right. You *wandered* in on your own, a guilty look on your face. You'd make a dreadful housebreaker or thief. Way too obvious."

Maybe it'd be better if he hadn't noticed me. Then I could hang out, watch The Merchants when they played later on, and enjoy the simple pleasures of life.

"Technically, I was on my own." I'd driven here myself after all. "But I'm not on my own anymore. I'm talking to you, and I've been mingling and being a very well behaved guest." I slumped against the counter. "Why would you want to make me feel bad?"

"I don't."

He reached for my arm, gave it a quick rub, more friendly than suggestive yet somehow it sent a tingle up my spine. I didn't need this, didn't need his attention, and sure as hell didn't need to be reminded about anything that'd happened before.

"I was enjoying teasing you," he said.

Meanwhile I couldn't understand why he made me feel so mixed up, so defensive, so many things all at once.

"I'm not sure what's going on here," I said. "Or maybe I'm reading too much into it. You accuse me of poisoning you when I never even said thirty was old. Because it isn't. And somehow I end up being partway between your grandmother and a cat burglar."

His eyebrows went up in the middle. "Sorry, that's not how I intended any of this."

I placed a hand on my chest. "Well, I'm not the one being a Mr. Poo Poo."

A second's silence, then he burst out laughing. "I've been called a lot of things in my time but never Mr. Poo Poo."

I couldn't back out now, not after I'd said something so stupid. "I like to tell it like it is."

"Maybe more people should do that. Don't move." He stepped to one side where he reached for a clean glass from the island counter, picked up an open bottle from the ice bucket, and poured me a glass of champagne. The expensive stuff, of course.

He handed me the glass. "Here you go. I'm going to tell it like it is too, so there's no misunderstanding. You're welcome to stay as long as you like. Have a drink. Have another."

What a guy. Maybe I had him all wrong. I sipped the champagne. Magnificent. So much nicer than the cheap stuff I drank with the girls and I appreciated it all the more because this drink, my second, would be my last. The downside of driving.

"I don't usually accept a drink unless I've seen the bottle being opened," I said. "It's one of those things."

"What things?"

"Like not drinking from a glass you've left unattended. Lots of girls are careful like that. Or at least I think they are."

"Always better to be cautious but I don't think there's too much to worry about tonight. Look, I'll join you." He poured himself a glass and had a drink.

"Sorry, I didn't mean to imply you were some kind of stalker or poisoner. It's just that it's different when you're a girl. Guys don't need to watch what they wear or how much they drink. They don't check the back seat before getting into the car or lock the doors as soon as they get in, especially at night."

I'd learned a lot from my bodyguard friend, Jess, over the years and had made a few mistakes along the way too, especially with drinking too much on occasion. Yet another learning experience.

"Maybe you're right," he said. "I hadn't thought of it that way."

"Don't you have sisters?"

"Just a brother."

I sipped my champagne. "Very nice. Far as I can tell, it's not spiked. Or poisoned."

"Yep, you've got to watch out for that." Morgan leaned closer. "You know this is the longest conversation we've had in years."

Years? He remembered. Anxiety simmered in my stomach. I shouldn't blame him for my own stupidity. But maybe I did, just a little.

I edged away. "Yes, that was a long time. An eon. An echelon."

He frowned. "An echelon?"

"That's what I said."

"An echelon is a level or rank. It doesn't have anything to do with time."

"I know that." My eyes narrowed. "Are you trying to make me look bad by pointing it out?"

He chuckled. "Holly, you're so funny."

"I wasn't trying to be funny."

"And that's exactly what makes it so amusing."

"I don't think you'll be laughing for very long."

"Why's that?"

"Chances are you're going to be seeing more of me." I cleared my throat. "We're going to be neighbors."

"What?"

"Next door neighbors."

The smile left his face. "You're kidding. I know my neighbors and neither of them has their house on the market."

"But the Ashtons are going to Europe for three months."

"Y-yes, they are." I could practically see the cogs in his head turning. "Don't tell me."

I gave him a little wave. "Yep, meet their new house sitter."

After Jess had told me Morgan's address and I'd worked this out, I'd had a bit of a panic, but I'd become used to the idea since then.

Besides, he'd be in his house and I'd be in mine. What could go wrong?